P9-DEV-264

A Five-Star Family Reunion

Just in time for Christmas!

The Pearson family promised their late mother that no matter what, they would *always* spend Christmas together. However, it has been three years and their special tradition is almost lost and forgotten...

Chiara has been traveling the world, but she's running out of money and needs help to get home. Meanwhile, Marco has been busy expanding the family hotel business in Europe, and *unexpectedly* expanding the family too. Having insisted his children make it back by Christmas Eve, Joshua has been preparing their Vermont cabin, until the arrival of his beautiful neighbor puts a wrench in the works...

Whatever it takes, the Pearson family *will* spend Christmas together this year!

Find out more in
Chiara and Evan's story
Wearing His Ring till Christmas
by Nina Singh

Marco and Eleanora's story
One-Night Baby to Christmas Proposal
by Susan Meier

and

Joshua and Rebecca's story
Christmas with His Ballerina
by Jessica Gilmore

Available now!

Dear Reader,

What a wonderful privilege it was to be part of A Five-Star Family Reunion. The three main characters—Joshua and his children, Chiara and Marco—had scattered to the four winds after the death of their family's matriarch.

Getting together for Christmas for the first time in years is their chance to heal their family. But discovering he'd fathered a child with his best friend has shattered Marco's life plan and jeopardized his goal of getting to the family cabin in Vermont for the reunion the family needs.

Eleanora DeLuca might have been childhood best friends with Marco, but she hadn't expected to be navigating a surprise pregnancy as she tries to ensure Marco arrives in Vermont for the Pearson Christmas Eve celebration. She worries so much about Marco that she doesn't guard her heart and before she knows it, she's in love with a guy who has vowed never to settle down.

But Christmas has a way of making magic. And Marco might have to fight harder than he thinks not to fall in love...

Grab a cup of cocoa and maybe a candy cane, and settle in for this beautiful story of unexpected love.

Susan Meier

One-Night Baby to Christmas Proposal

Susan Meier

———

If you purchased this book without a cover you should be aware
that this book is stolen property. It was reported as "unsold and
destroyed" to the publisher, and neither the author nor the
publisher has received any payment for this "stripped book."

Special thanks and acknowledgment are given to Susan Meier
for her contribution to A Five-Star Family Reunion miniseries.

Recycling programs
for this product may
not exist in your area.

ISBN-13: 978-1-335-73688-8

One-Night Baby to Christmas Proposal

Copyright © 2022 by Harlequin Enterprises ULC

All rights reserved. No part of this book may be used or reproduced in
any manner whatsoever without written permission except in the case of
brief quotations embodied in critical articles and reviews.

This is a work of fiction. Names, characters, places and incidents
are either the product of the author's imagination or are used fictitiously.
Any resemblance to actual persons, living or dead, businesses,
companies, events or locales is entirely coincidental.

For questions and comments about the quality of this book,
please contact us at CustomerService@Harlequin.com.

Harlequin Enterprises ULC
22 Adelaide St. West, 41st Floor
Toronto, Ontario M5H 4E3, Canada
www.Harlequin.com

Printed in U.S.A.

Susan Meier is the author of over fifty books for Harlequin. *The Tycoon's Secret Daughter* was a Romance Writers of America RITA® Award finalist, and *Nanny for the Millionaire's Twins* won the Book Buyers Best Award and was a finalist in the National Readers' Choice Awards. Susan is married and has three children. One of eleven children herself, she loves to write about the complexity of families and totally believes in the power of love.

Books by Susan Meier

Harlequin Romance

Scandal at the Palace

His Majesty's Forbidden Fling

A Billion-Dollar Family

Tuscan Summer with the Billionaire
The Billionaire's Island Reunion
The Single Dad's Italian Invitation

Christmas at the Harrington Park Hotel

Stolen Kiss with Her Billionaire Boss

Hired by the Unexpected Billionaire
Reunited Under the Mistletoe

Visit the Author Profile page
at Harlequin.com for more titles.

To Skoda and Mobi, Nancy Herkness's cats, the inspiration for Sunrise and Sunset. They might not be orange, but they were the curious and funny example I used to create my two fun felines.

Praise for Susan Meier

"The perfect choice. I read this in one sitting; once I started, I couldn't put it down. *The Bodyguard and the Heiress* will put a smile in your heart. What I love most about Susan Meier's books is the joy your heart feels as you take the journey with characters that come to life. Love this book."

—*Goodreads*

CHAPTER ONE

COULD THERE BE anything more embarrassing than being pregnant by a man who wishes he hadn't slept with you?

Actually, there could be if he was your boss—

And your childhood friend.

Eleanora DeLuca stared at the pregnancy test stick, not sure if she should groan in disbelief or complete panic.

August 24 had been the best day of her life, celebrating the grand opening of her hotel—

Well, it wasn't really *her* hotel. It belonged to the Grand York Hotel Group. She was simply the manager of their Rome offering, the Group's first ever international hotel, the beginning of a new chapter in the company's history. It was an honor to be given the job, an honor to have the opportunity to put her stamp on every detail and she'd had her share of champagne to celebrate it.

But the best part of the night had been finally

getting the attention of her longtime friend and forever crush, Marco Pearson, her boss and one of the people who owned the Grand York Hotel Group. They'd kissed and teased their way to the suite reserved for her that night and made love like two people starving for the taste of each other. But the next day she'd awakened alone.

When she arrived at her first-floor office, she'd been told Marco had returned to Manhattan, and when he'd called her a few days later, he'd told her that sleeping together had been a mistake. Not because he disliked her. Exactly the opposite. Their friendship spanned two and a half decades. He didn't want to lose that. He wanted to go back to being just friends.

She squeezed her eyes shut. She was pregnant by her boss.

A guy who wished they hadn't slept together.

He was smart and sophisticated, the kind of man who dated movie stars and social media influencers.

And she was carrying his child?

The universe had certainly gotten this one wrong.

She dropped her head to her free hand and groaned.

In the grand scheme of things, her life was a

study in Murphy's Law. If something could go wrong, it did.

Her personal phone rang. She lifted it from her bedside table and groaned again.

The man of her dreams, father of her child, guy who wished he hadn't slept with her was calling.

She took a breath and answered. "Good morning, Marco."

"What's up? I tried to reach you on your work phone, and you didn't pick up."

She could picture him sitting behind his big desk in the Manhattan offices of the Grand York Hotel Group. His short black hair would be neatly combed. Tall and athletic, he'd look like the perfect businessman in his dark suit with sedate print tie. But she'd seen what was beneath his stately clothes. She'd touched the muscles, traced her tongue along the indentations defining his pecs.

She'd heard him laugh. She'd *made* him laugh. And she'd also made him moan with pleasure.

Longing and confusion whispered through her. She was strong enough, *smart enough*, not to yearn for something she couldn't have. A pregnancy would not change his feelings about their relationship.

And if it did, would she want that?

Would she want the man who'd already admitted sleeping with her had been a mistake to change his feelings for her because she was carrying his child?

No.

This was awful—a mess that didn't just encompass her personal life; it dragged in her work life too. And she wasn't ready to be chipper, happy, Eleanora, the perfect employee. She would need a couple of hours to adjust to being pregnant before she could talk business. "I'm a little under the weather today."

"I'm sorry! You're sick and I'm bugging you about work. I'll hang up—"

On the other hand, she also didn't want to jeopardize her job or make him think she wasn't strong enough to handle it.

"I woke up with a headache this morning." Dropping the pregnancy test in the trash, she winced at the lie. She never lied. And that was the second part of her problem. She would not lie to him about being her baby's father. But it was already October 24, two months into her pregnancy. If she didn't tell him within the next couple of weeks, he would notice her baby bump when she began to show and that could get even messier. Meaning, she had to tell him soon—

But not today. Right now, she was not up to facing the truth with him. If a little white lie bought her some time, she would cross her fingers behind her back as she said it.

"I'll take a few painkillers and be in the office in about an hour. You can call me then."

"You're sure you're okay? You don't think you need to see a doctor?"

She shook her head in wonder that someone who was so smart, so observant, so kind and caring, could miss that she was hedging. But they had been friends forever. His concern for her as his friend would trump everything else and he'd assume that role, rather than speak to her as her boss.

"I'm sure." She took another long, slow breath. "As I said, I'll be in my office in an hour. We can discuss anything you want."

"Actually, I just wanted to remind you that I'll be in Rome next week."

She managed to hold back a groan, but that only resulted in apprehension vibrating through her voice. "Oh, I haven't forgotten."

He laughed. "It's not like you to fear a visit from the boss. I'm guessing every lamp is polished and every piece of silver sparkles. I can't imagine you'd have anything to worry about."

Only a pregnancy.

But that was a discussion for next week.

She had seven whole days to decide what she

wanted to do, what she wanted to say and how she'd say it.

"Goodbye, Marco. If there's nothing else you need, I'll be available in an hour."

"Don't forget the painkillers."

She grimaced. "I won't."

Marco Pearson hung up the phone and frowned. He had never heard Eleanora sound as…unprofessional?…as she had in that phone call. He leaned back in his office chair, swiveling it so he could see the jaw-dropping view of Manhattan behind him.

His elbow on the chair's arm, he ran his finger along his upper lip. Since the night of the grand opening for the Grand York Rome, he'd had flashes of memory of them together. First, dancing at the party in the ballroom. Then, laughing as they raced up the elaborate lobby stairs. Then a flash of her naked. Soft and pink. Her auburn hair disheveled. Her green eyes sparkling.

He'd never wanted a woman more. But sleeping with his best friend had been a huge mistake. They'd known each other since childhood. Navigated the lumps and bumps of high school together. She'd been his first hire, when his dad let him run the front desk at the original Grand York the summer after he'd graduated. He'd nursed her back to health after her first hangover. She'd helped him decipher the nuances of every job he'd held with the Grand York. She'd helped him through the trauma of losing his mom. He'd watched out for promotions that were good for her. *Their fathers were still friends.* A smart man did not jeopardize that kind of relationship over one night of sex.

Particularly since they knew each other's secrets and dreams and a bad breakup could be explosive—

Because he knew they'd break up eventually. Neither one of them had a good track record with relationships. She always seemed to end up with guys who weren't good for her, and he didn't believe in happily-ever-after. So technically that made him one of the guys who weren't good for her. He'd long ago vowed never to tie himself down. If he let this thing between them go on, the end could destroy at least her career and probably severely damage his.

Worse, their fathers might get involved.

Dear God.

He would not let that happen. A few days after they'd slept together, he'd told her what they'd had could go no further and she'd accepted it. Now, he intended to do damage control on his visit to Rome by showing her that nothing had changed between them.

They were still friends. They would always be friends. And they would never do *that* again.

No matter how much fun it had been.

He finished the week clearing up things that needed to be done before he left for Rome late Monday night. As he walked up the steps of the family's private jet, dread tiptoed through him. There had been no tabloid article about him making a spectacle of himself in Rome the night of the grand opening. No employee gossip filtered to him about his inappropriate behavior. Because his behavior hadn't been inappropriate. He'd done nothing that would rouse anyone's suspicions.

Dancing with Eleanora wouldn't raise any red flags.

Racing up the stairs with her wouldn't either.

Everyone knew they were close friends. Everyone also knew the party had been about celebrating. Everyone had had too much champagne. Everyone had laughed and danced and in general enjoyed themselves.

As long as he and Eleanora had been laughing, invited guests of the hotel would have simply seen two friends having fun.

No one would have guessed they'd gone to her room and made love.

But none of that really mattered. It was his friendship with Eleanora he was worried about.

What if she'd said she was fine pretending nothing had happened between them, when she really wasn't?

Their phone conversation the week before rose in his thoughts. She wasn't prone to headaches. So maybe she'd given him the bum's rush because she didn't want to talk to him?

He lowered himself to his seat and buckled in, wincing at that possibility. She could very well be upset and pretending she wasn't to keep peace between them to protect her job.

As planned, he slept through the long flight and only woke when the copilot's voice burst into the main cabin announcing they were preparing to land. A glance at his watch told him it was almost noon in Italy. With another yawn, he gathered his wits as the family's private jet landed.

Jogging down the six steps from the plane to the tarmac, he looked over to see the black limo awaiting him. But his eyebrows rose when he saw Eleanora leaning against the fender beside the back door. As he walked to the vehicle, she pushed away from the car.

"Good morning."

"Good morning to you too." Normally, having her meet him would have made him smile. But this wasn't usual protocol. Given that she hadn't mentioned meeting him, he assumed she was taking this opportunity to discuss something privately. A perfectly normal thing for a new hotel manager.

Or a woman who wanted to have it out with him.

Though the decision to make love that night had been mutual—neither was too impaired to make the choice—he was her boss. He was supposed to be smarter than to be seduced by or seduce an employee. She wouldn't sue him. But she might call a halt to their friendship. Then he'd have to explain to his dad. And his dad might face questions from the DeLuca family—

He prayed she simply wanted to discuss something about the hotel. "To what do I owe the pleasure of you meeting me?"

The driver opened the back door and Marco motioned for Eleanora to enter first.

"There are a few things we need to discuss, and I wanted privacy."

That was what he expected, but his brain jumped back to the grand opening and their blissful night together, and his gut tightened. He stopped that reaction, telling himself that his *manager* most likely wanted to discuss the hotel.

He got into the limo. The door closed behind him. She raised the privacy glass.

Oh, God. She wanted to end their friendship. He was going to have to explain to his dad that he'd slept with her—the daughter of his friend, a woman Joshua Pearson treated like a daughter.

She glanced at him with an awkward smile, and he readied himself. They were friends. He would fix this. He would not let her end their friendship.

"I'm pregnant."

Shock made his mind go blank. "What?"

The limo began to navigate the tarmac to get to the road out of the airport.

"I know you wanted us to just forget we slept together after the grand opening celebration… and, honestly, I could have done that if that was how you wanted it—"

He stared at her. How *he* wanted it? She hadn't wanted to forget they'd slept together? What had she expected to happen? That they'd begin a relationship?

He shook himself back to reality. None of that mattered! He had to deal with one problem at a time. She was *pregnant*. How he handled getting the news could determine the future of their friendship—

And their work relationship.

Oh, God. This pregnancy would play out in front of the employees of the Rome hotel, as well as the employees of the corporate office. There would be jokes and teasing. Water-cooler gossip.

Once again, that didn't matter. He was an adult. He could survive a little teasing.

So could she.

But it sounded like they needed to be honest right now. As honest as they'd always been with each other.

He took a breath. "Okay. First, I'm sorry that things at the grand opening ended up with us sleeping together. I want to blame alcohol."

"I want to blame alcohol too, but neither one of us was drunk." She paused for a quick drink of air. "Look, we were having fun. We'd worked hard on getting the hotel done and open. We simply didn't think ahead to potential consequences."

Those consequences rumbled through his brain, making him tingle with confusion. "A baby."

She caught his gaze. "Yeah."

His entire body went numb, as a million thoughts bombarded him. Scary thoughts. Overwhelming thoughts. Not just diapers and bottles, but swing sets and grammar school, teen years, university, things he never thought about because he'd never even considered becoming a dad.

Never.

They fell silent. He didn't know why she was quiet except she probably had an equal number of scary, overwhelming thoughts. And, clearly, neither one of them had any answers.

If he'd worried making love would impact their friendship, becoming parents had a million even more drastic potential consequences.

On the seemingly endless drive to Rome's Grand York Hotel, the idea tiptoed into his mind that they should get married, but his soul roared with refusal.

Roared.

Marriage?

That wasn't who he was. First, being unencumbered made it possible for him to be the best Managing Director of the family's hotel chain that he could be. Second, he watched his father mourn his mom after her death and become a completely different person. Even a love as strong as his parents', a love that seemed like it would last forever, had ended when his mother died, proving there was no such thing as happily-ever-after. A person was a fool to buy into that.

But he knew Eleanora. He knew she wanted the fairy tale, even if it meant being disillusioned by it at some point.

He wouldn't ask her to marry him. Not merely because he didn't believe in marriage, but also to leave her free to pursue marriage if she wanted it.

One thing decided. But so many others

crowded his brain. Back to bottles and diapers. Learning to walk. Custody. Visitation. He'd have to hire a nanny. Did nannies work part-time? Like only for visitation? Could he keep his penthouse? How the hell did someone baby-proof a home?

He was going to be a terrible father!

They walked into Rome's Grand York Hotel and everyone from the bellboys to the registration desk employees welcomed him with broad smiles. Who could blame them? They were all part of something extraordinary. A gorgeous hotel, made for pampering people. They worked as a team, like a family.

He glanced around at the high ceilings of the lobby, the elegant corbels in corners and the dark cherrywood reception area that shone from a recent polishing, then his gaze was drawn to the stunning circular stairway that led to the mezzanine and a bank of elevators that went to ultra-expensive, ultra-private rooms. He remembered racing up that stairway with Eleanora. He could all but see it in his mind's eye and almost hear the way their laughter rang along the high ceilings.

The reception clerks all said hello. A bellboy tipped his hat. No one treated him oddly. Gracious manager that she was, Eleanora stood tall and elegant in her white dress and navy blue high heels, her auburn hair curling around her shoulders.

While he was churning inside, remembering a night that resulted in his becoming a father, she was perfectly calm.

But she'd had time to process this. He hadn't. Too much was at stake here for him not to step away and think this through before they talked any more.

The desk clerk gave him the key to the exclusive penthouse. "Thank you."

He turned away from the desk, caught Eleanora's upper arm and eased them away from everybody before he quietly said, "I'm sorry to bail on you today, but what you told me in the car was the absolute last thing I expected to hear."

Obviously aware of the employees around them, she didn't say anything, didn't mention the pregnancy, only inclined her head to indicate she understood.

"I won't be in the office this afternoon. I'll be in my room. Please don't take offense, but I need to process this."

With that he walked to the elevator, got in, pressed in the code for the penthouse suite and left.

CHAPTER TWO

WATCHING HIM GO, Eleanora stood in the lobby, smiling her most professional smile, then she walked into her office and flopped down into her desk chair. He hadn't been happy, but his reaction hadn't been god-awful either. She'd needed the day to sort her thoughts after she'd seen the positive pregnancy test. She'd give him the same consideration.

What she hadn't expected was her reaction to being with him in the lobby of the Grand York Rome. The second they'd stepped inside, it was as if her body became hyperaware of his. Desire had flooded her. Memories of their night together filled her brain with pictures of touching him and being touched by him, falling asleep tucked into his side—

And waking to find him gone. She couldn't forget that.

She'd thought his decisive proclamation that he wanted nothing to do with her would have splashed a bucket of cold water on her attraction, but obviously her hormones had a mind of their own. She either had to figure out a way to shut them down or drown them out when she and Marco met the next morning to talk about the hotel.

Wednesday, she dressed in a sedate black dress that hugged her curves. She frowned when she looked at herself in the mirror. The tiny waist she loved so much, the curvy but toned body she worked so hard to maintain, was about to explode as their baby grew inside her.

She told herself not to panic. She was a little over eight weeks pregnant. Her tummy was still flat. So far, she hadn't had any morning sickness. No one would be able to tell she was pregnant.

But when they did, there would be whispers.

She shook her head. Once again, that was a problem for another day. Unless she or Marco said or did something foolish, there would be no whispers today. And she fully intended to keep control of herself, her emotions and especially those damned hormones that kept reminding her of kissing him and—other things.

After a few breaths to compose herself, she slid into her snakeskin high-heel sandals and headed out of her apartment to her small car and to the Grand York Hotel.

Wearing her sunglasses, she walked into the

lobby. Her pride in what she and Marco had accomplished showed in her wide smile and confident stride. She had months before she lost her waist and even more months until she had to take time off, have the baby, find childcare. She should enjoy these months—

Except, the planner in her wouldn't let her ignore the fact that she was pregnant. It kicked into high gear, filling her head with a to-do list. To keep the job she loved, she'd need a nanny. Eventually, she'd need a bigger apartment. She'd have to decide if she'd breastfeed. And if she did, she'd have to learn how to use a breast pump. Then there were bottles and diapers, nanny cams and baby monitors—

Telling her parents.

The urge to hyperventilate raced through her and she stopped.

Stopped walking.

Stopped the long list of things mounting in her brain.

Because no matter how much her inner planner wanted to be let loose on some of these items, today was not the day to start any of them. Today she had to meet with Marco, see how he was handling this and answer his questions. Or maybe hope he would want to talk about the hotel, the reasons for his visit, and let the other stuff settle for another few days.

Standing by the registration area, reading something on his phone, Marco didn't see her, but she saw him. Gorgeous, talented, smart, fun-loving Marco. Looking at him always made her heart skip a beat, but now the feelings were different, stronger. All because her fantasy had come to life, and she knew he really was as sensational in bed as she'd always dreamed he'd be.

Her heart thrummed, but she reminded herself that she'd decided to get control of herself and keep control.

She headed toward the registration area, her head high, her breathing steady. Marco didn't even look up until she was right beside him.

He started. "Oh! Eleanora!"

She pulled down her sunglasses. "What's on the agenda for today?"

"Lots. But first… Have you eaten?"

She frowned. "What?"

"Eaten? Breakfast?"

His comment confused her. But so did his calm. Here she was struggling with the longing to slide her arms around him and kiss him and he was worried about food? "No. I don't usually eat breakfast, but if you want to go to the restaurant and begin our discussions there, I'm fine with that."

"You need breakfast."

"I'm not hungry."

He lowered his voice. "What if the baby is?"

Her breathing stopped. The last thing they needed was one of the employees overhearing this discussion. She directed him away from the reception desk. "What's going on here?"

"I'm just…you know…looking out for you."

The thought was sweet, vintage Marco, but having him hover over her was the last thing she needed. If he was too nice, too kind, she'd fall hopelessly in love.

"Okay. First, I don't need any help taking care of myself. Second, the lobby is the wrong place to talk about any of this. Let's get some coffee."

She turned him to the left and walked him to the restaurant. Dark wood chairs surrounded round tables covered in white linen tablecloths. Gino, the maître d', snapped to attention.

"Good morning!"

"Good morning, Gino," she said pleasantly. "Mr. Pearson and I would like a table over there." She pointed at a space with empty tables. "And keep it private. Don't seat anyone near us."

"Yes, ma'am," Gino said, leading them to the table.

After they settled on their seats, Gino promised to return with a pot of coffee. Eleanora smiled and let him scamper away.

"You can't have coffee."

Eleanora sighed, "Did you spend the night Googling pregnancy?"

"I might have looked up a few things."

Gino returned with the silver tea service, and two delicate cups and saucers. Marco ordered eggs, bacon and toast and Eleanora pointedly told Gino she only wanted a glass of water.

When he was gone, Marco sighed. "You have to eat."

The guy was the sexiest, most considerate man in the world. Having him care about her, somehow made him sexier. But she saw two waitresses open the door of the kitchen a crack and peek at them. Her gut reaction was to walk over and tell them to stop being nosy and get back to work, then she realized they could be looking at the tables, the customers, or discussing how they'd handle the lunch rush, almost anything.

Telling herself to get her head in the game, she faced Marco again. "According to what I've read, I need to keep up my typical eating habits. When the baby needs more sustenance, I will get hungrier."

He frowned.

"We haven't even started discussing things like when and how we'll tell our families, custody, visitation, how involved *you* want to be. If we get hung up on things like when I eat, we'll never get to the important decisions."

"I guess."

"*I know.* Plus, I'm an adult, someone you consider smart enough to run your first international hotel. It seems to me that you should be able to trust me to pick my own meals."

She reached for the coffeepot. "Not only that but I read that I can have one cup of coffee a day." She poured a cup of coffee but handed it to him. "But I've decided to abstain."

He took a quick breath. "Okay. I'm sorry."

"Marco, we've always been able to separate our friendship from our work. Let's do that with this too."

His eggs and bacon arrived. She sipped her water. A bellboy and a registration desk clerk walked by the glass wall in front of the restaurant. Though they tried to be casual, both looked in at the same time. They craned their necks to see beyond the front tables—

Because she and Marco were in the back?

There might not be whispers about her pregnancy but there were definitely whispers about *her and Marco.* This was the first time they'd been together since the grand opening. She and Marco hadn't been discreet that night as they'd danced and raced up the grand staircase in the lobby together, and God only knew if anyone had seen him going into her room with her.

Setting his linen napkin on his lap, Marco pulled back his annoyance that she wasn't eating. She was correct. She was an adult. She was intelligent. She would do the right things.

She set her water on the table in front of her, as she leaned back in her chair, craning her neck to look through the glass into the hall off the lobby. The neat little black dress she wore outlined her curves nicely. The way she was sitting drew his attention to her chest. He remembered touching her, pressing her up against the wall by the door in her room. The flash of memory came with a jolt of attraction that sent shivers along his spine. Making love with her had been—

Breathtakingly sensual.

And perhaps this was not the best time to remember that.

He quickly shifted his attention to his eggs. "So...no morning sickness?"

She turned to look at him. "Not yet."

"That's good."

"It is."

The conversation died and her scent drifted to him. As friends, he had barely ever noticed it. But the olfactory nerve was the devil. The second her scent touched it, a million sensations fired off. Pleasure. Happiness. Hunger and need.

He didn't see a picture of that night, the way he had when he looked at the stairway. He didn't remember anything being said. Just sensations that stole his breath and made him want to—

He choked on his eggs.

What was he doing! *Eleanora was his friend.* Who was also an employee and a friend of his father's! They might have had one night of passion—made one mistake—but he wouldn't compound it by repeating it. Those urges prompted by the sensations he kept feeling…? They were wrong.

He took a long sip of water, then glanced at Eleanora. "I guess the first thing we need to talk about is when we will be telling people."

"I've decided not to tell anyone at the hotel until I have to." She glanced at the door, then returned her gaze to him. "But I want to tell my parents as soon as possible."

He peered over at her. "As soon as possible?"

"It's always best not to keep secrets from your parents." She looked at the door again, then said, "You should tell your dad soon too."

The mention of his dad threw his nervous system into overdrive. Not only did he have to get accustomed to the idea of being a father, with a woman who worked for him, and was also his friend, but he'd promised his dad he would spend the holiday with him—beginning on December 23. He didn't want the holiday celebration—the first time he, his dad and his sister spent Christmas together in three years—to be ruined by the announcement that he'd slept with Eleanora.

She was right. The sooner he told his dad the better—

Picturing the scene, with his dad expressing his disappointment in him and wanting him to marry Eleanora, a woman he loved like a daughter, Marco almost closed his eyes in despair. The last thing he wanted to do was explain to his dad that he didn't want to get married because he didn't believe in love. After the death of his mom, Marco was certain his dad agreed with him, but he didn't want to say the words, to talk about the loss that hung over their heads every damned day. His mom had been wonderful, a gift from God, and losing her ten years ago had not been easy.

Still, surely, he could tell his dad in such a way that talk of marriage never came into it? Maybe with time? Maybe it would be better to wait until he was adjusted before he tried to explain to his dad?

"I think I need to get accustomed to the idea before I tell anyone."

"I understand."

He shook his head. "And I wish you didn't." Except for the way she kept glancing at the door, she was cool, calm, collected. "I wish you'd be nervous or upset or anxious or at least as overwhelmed as I am."

She smiled at him. "Who says I'm not?"

Her smile threw him for a loop, stalling his breath. She was the consummate professional, but today everything about her was infused with femininity. It was like she was so pretty, so sexy in the slim black dress that she couldn't hide it.

And noticing that was wrong!

He cleared his throat. "You don't look anxious or overwhelmed." She looked like someone a man would crawl across a bed for. And if he remembered correctly, he had.

She laughed. "One of us has to keep their wits."

Clearly, it wasn't going to be him. At least not until he got himself acclimated to their predicament. It had to be their night of passion that had his hormones so attuned to her. But the reason didn't matter. He needed to get a hold of himself.

His appetite suddenly gone, he set his napkin on the table. "All right. I get it. You're teasing me."

"You're not taking this very well."

"I'm just surprised. There I was expecting

you to tell me everything between us changed because we'd slept together, and you tell me that you're pregnant."

"Same thing, if you think about it."

Marco rolled his eyes. "Not really."

"This isn't the end of the world, Marco. It's a shift in our lives."

She didn't have any idea how big of a shift this was for him. He didn't believe in marriage. He'd never even considered being a father. The woman he accidentally impregnated was a woman he admired as an employee and treasured as a friend. His entire life felt like a puzzle that had been taken apart and the pieces strewn across a table with no rhyme or reason and no clue about how to put them back together.

Worse, there was a lot at stake. If he didn't handle this right, he could lose her as a friend, maybe even an employee. And no matter what he decided, his dad wasn't going to take this well.

After a quick tour of the conference areas, a few of the guest suites and the kitchen—where the chef almost fainted with happiness over his being there—they walked through the lobby and down the long silent hall to the hotel's offices.

The second they stepped into the workspace of Eleanora's assistant, Sheila jumped from her desk chair.

"Good morning, Marco!"

"Good morning, Sheila." In their one hour of touring the hotel, his voice had lost its nervous edge. He sounded normal again. Meaning, he was adjusting to the news already. Surely, things would continue to get better.

Eleanora said, "Good morning, Sheila," then led Marco into her office.

As he followed her, his gaze cruised down her back and to her bottom. Just as it had in the restaurant, his entire body sizzled. He almost groaned. He might be adjusting to the news that he was about to become a father, but his hormones refused to behave around Eleanora. He told himself he should have kept his eyes up, but he seemed to have no control around her anymore.

She walked to her desk, grabbed a stack of reports, and ambled to the conference table. A pile of files about the size of what she had in her arms sat in front of the chair at the head of the table. She took the seat on the right. Leaving the seat of command for him.

Desperate to get down to business and forget everything else, he walked over, removed his jacket and sat down. "What have we here?"

"I thought we'd take a look at the expenses

for each individual department before we get into big picture numbers."

"Sounds good."

He picked up the top report as she opened her top report. Her hands were small, but her fingers were long, the nails painted a soft gray. He stopped his brain before it could form an inappropriate memory about those nails scraping down his back. He managed to get through ten minutes of her listing her expenses, but that was it. The past eight weeks, he'd blocked all thoughts of their night together. But being with her had memories cascading through him uncontrollably. He swore his body had some sort of muscle memories because certain things caused his chest to tighten or his breath to stutter.

After one particularly interesting memory, he jumped from his chair. "You know what? I think that's enough for this morning."

She glanced at her watch. "It's not even eleven." She frowned. "Do you want lunch?"

He didn't. He was still full from breakfast. But *she* hadn't eaten. "I'm not sure." Dismayed at his inability to form coherent thought, he sat again. "I mean... Aren't *you* hungry?"

She sighed and closed the report she'd been referencing. "Marco, you have to settle down."

Glad she thought it was the pregnancy and

not unexpectedly clear memories of their night together that had him so flummoxed, he said, "I am… I *will*. I just think it'll take a few days for the pregnancy to sink in."

Sheila cleared her throat. Marco's gaze jumped to the door where she stood, her face red, her expression apologetic.

"I'm sorry, Eleanora. Your parents called on the hotel line. They said they couldn't get an answer on your cell phone, so they tried this number."

Marco caught Eleanora's gaze. He knew what they both were thinking. Sheila had heard his last comment.

She took a breath, then broke their eye contact to address Sheila. "Are they on the line now?"

Sheila nodded.

"Okay. I'll pick up."

Looking eternally grateful, Sheila nodded again and raced from the room.

As Eleanora walked to her desk, Marco sighed. "You know that if I close the door now, she's going to guess we were talking about your—*our* being pregnant."

"It doesn't matter. In an hour, that word *pregnancy* will have traveled through the entire hotel and speculation will be everything from the guess that *we're* pregnant, or *you* got some-

body pregnant, or somebody got *me* pregnant."
She reached for the phone but didn't pick it up.
"We're good enough friends that everybody
knows I'd tell you if I was pregnant or you'd
tell me if you'd gotten somebody pregnant." Her
head tilted. "That would probably be their first
guess rather than that *we're* pregnant. Actually,
I think we're safe. Because anything they guess
will be a guess and everybody will treat it like
gossip."

She lifted the phone's receiver. "Mom?" Listening as her mom spoke, she laughed and sat
on the big chair behind the desk.

Marco looked skyward. Though he wanted to
groan, his common sense told him there was no
point in hiding the pregnancy or the fact that he
was the baby's father. Everything would come
out eventually. Plus, he'd already decided he
could handle a little ribbing.

But watching Eleanora talk to her mom, the
way she kept hedging, he knew she needed to
tell her parents sooner rather than later. And
he had to tell his dad before something leaked
through the corporate grapevine. Which was
probably why Eleanora had told him at breakfast that he should tell his dad soon.

Plus, they had a million things to decide. Custody. Visitation. His involvement. How involved

could he be when she lived in Rome, and he lived in New York? There'd be discussions of baby names, schools, holidays, vacations, even what the poor kid would wear.

He suddenly realized that the reason he was so antsy, so jumpy, so befuddled was because he was a person of action. He did not sit on problems. He solved them.

Being here, pretending nothing was wrong, putting something else ahead of the biggest thing to happen in his personal life since the death of his mom? That's what was making him crazy.

She hung up the phone. "My mother's nuts. She's making plans for Christmas because I promised I would be home. It's only the beginning of November and she's working on a menu for a holiday that's weeks away."

"I think we should leave—go home."

She frowned. "To my apartment?"

"No. Home. Home. I need—*we* need—to figure out some things, make plans, make decisions, tell people. I don't want to waste a week in Rome talking about work, then go back to Manhattan as if nothing's different." He caught her gaze. "*Everything's* different. And I need to figure some of this out."

She rose behind the desk. "Okay. Go home."

"Oh, no. I'm not going alone. You're coming with me. This is about both of us. We need to make these decisions together. We need to do this right, or it might cost us our friendship."

She took a breath, thinking through what he'd said. His heart tweaked a bit with worry that she didn't consider their friendship as important as he did.

But she suddenly shrugged and said, "You know what? You're right. This might be a make or break for us. If we want to keep our friendship, we need to do this correctly."

Relief billowed through him.

"Plus, it will be good to tell my parents in person."

"Yes! That's it exactly!" The relief that had gone through him turned to happiness. The whole battery of odd thoughts he'd been having around her really had been nothing but his brain rebelling with confusion over letting a problem hang over his head. Now, that they were taking steps to solve it, he could breathe again, think normally again.

Then she stepped out from behind the desk and everything about her from her soft red-brown hair to her sexy high heels hit him like a punch in the gut. Feelings fluttered in his stomach. His muscles tightened.

He wished with all his might that he could forget their night together, then decided that taking her to New York, spending a week or so with her, might be the way to get so accustomed to her that the memories had no power.

CHAPTER THREE

WALKING ELEANORA TO her car at the end of the day, Marco texted his sister. "I'm just letting Chiara know I'll be back in New York in case she needs me."

Eleanora nodded and smiled. On a normal visit, it wouldn't surprise her that Marco would walk her to her car, but his overprotectiveness that morning at breakfast added to his weird reactions about the baby were beginning to concern her.

"We both decided to go to the family cabin in Vermont for Christmas with Dad, and it almost seems like our texts are a way of ensuring the other doesn't bail."

She glanced at the umbrella pines that lined the parking lot, inhaling the still-warm November air, as she walked the last few feet to her car. "Are you planning on bailing?"

"No. But that's the point. We talked about going there every year for the past three years, but always find a reason not to go." He paused as if considering his next words, but eventually shook his head and said, "I think it just reminds us all of Mom's death."

"Oh, Marco! I'm so sorry. I should have thought before I asked."

"No. No. It's fine." He looked up at the pretty blue sky. "It's not like we've been stagnating." He glanced back at the lush hotel and his face shifted from unhappy to happy in the blink of an eye. "We've accomplished a lot."

"Yes, you have."

"But lately we seem to scatter at Christmas."

She nodded at his phone. "Looks like this year will be different."

"Let's hope."

He reached around her to open her car door. "I'll call tonight with specifics about our trip home tomorrow once I arrange things with the pilots. I should have my assistant do it but keeping busy is good for me right now."

She smiled in agreement, got into her car and said, "Goodbye. See you tomorrow."

He said, "See you tomorrow," then stepped back to let her pull out.

The way he watched her as she drove off made her take a long drink of air. She knew he and his family hadn't had Christmas together for a few years, but she hadn't taken the timing into consideration when she told him they were pregnant. They'd slept together in late August. The months that had passed before she'd taken the pregnancy test had been too busy to think about an upcoming holiday. Plus, it was still warm. With the exception of telling her parents she would visit for the holiday, she wasn't thinking about Christmas yet.

But he was. And getting together with his father and sister clearly upset him—and his sister. If he was worried that she would bail, he must have his suspicions.

No wonder he was nervous and antsy and having trouble processing everything. From here on out she would be more careful how she presented things to him.

Glad he'd left her alone that night, so she'd have some time to think about things as she packed, she headed into her apartment. After dumping her purse on a convenient chair, she made herself a sandwich for dinner, then frowned at it. With the way Marco watched her, that sandwich would probably be the last normal supper she'd be getting for a while.

She finished eating and was going to shower but decided to get her suitcase off the dusty closet shelf before she did. Using a small step stool, she reached up to get the suitcase. It slid off the shelf too quickly and she grabbed for it.

With one hand on the handle and the other bracing the body of the case, she tossed it to the floor.

A sharp pain pierced her belly. Clutching it, she gasped. But after a few seconds, the pain went away. A little more careful this time, she lifted the suitcase onto the bed and began packing. Halfway through, pain rippled through her belly again.

She stopped, put her hand on her lower abdomen. This pain was different.

She took a breath, then another. The pain lessened in severity until it went away.

Almost like a contraction.

Sitting on the bed, she squeezed her eyes shut. She had no idea what was normal and what wasn't in a pregnancy. When her sister went through this, she'd been hundreds of miles away in the Midwest while Eleanora had been in Manhattan. If she'd had troubles, she'd never spoken of them.

Of course, she might not have had troubles. Her pregnancies might have been normal—

Meaning, Eleanora's pregnancy *wasn't* normal?

With the pain gone and her head full of scary things, she pushed herself off the bed and gathered clothes for her trip. When her suitcase was packed, she headed for the shower. Nothing had happened in the hour it had taken her to pack.

The first pain could have been a muscle spasm from lifting the suitcase. The second one? It might have been nothing.

She stripped and was about to step into the shower when she realized there were droplets of blood in her panties.

She froze.

But she quickly realized that adding the pain and the blood, no matter how miniscule, meant something.

She raced into her bedroom, threw on sweat-pants and a T-shirt, slid into sandals and headed for the hospital. It was too late for a doctor's office to be open, but she also hadn't yet chosen an obstetrician. Besides, this problem seemed to call for a hospital.

She arrived and headed into the Emergency Department. As she rushed inside, butterflies filled her stomach. She really needed Marco right now. Attraction be damned. She was alone and scared, and he was the one she wanted at her side.

After registering at the front desk, she pulled out her phone. He answered on the first ring.

"Hey… I…um. I'm at the emergency room."

"What?"

She squeezed her eyes shut. She didn't want to rattle him. She didn't want to feed her attraction. She took a breath and tried to sound calm.

"I had a few things happen and decided to take precautions—"

He didn't even wait for her to finish. "What hospital?"

She told him the name of the hospital at the same time that a nurse called for her. She disconnected the call, and the nurse took her back to an exam room. After a fifteen-minute wait, a doctor gave her an exam and explained that some pain and even some spotting were normal. But to prove to her that everything was fine, he would do a scan.

Marco burst into the room just as the doctor began the scan.

The old man laughed. "I'm guessing you're the father?"

Out of breath, he raced to her side. "Yes! How is she?"

Eleanora said, "I'm fine," as the doctor said, "She's fine."

"The baby?"

"Fine too." The doctor pointed at the screen beside Eleanora's bed. "See?"

Eleanora glanced at the screen and saw a lot of blurry stuff and something that looked like a bean. But it was the sound of the heartbeat thrumming into the room that stole her breath. She'd always understood that pregnancy meant there was a child growing inside her, but hearing the heartbeat filled her with emotions she couldn't describe. Love came to mind. So did joy. But it went beyond that. The reality that that little bean was her child filled her with awe.

She blinked and caught Marco's hand. "Do you hear that?"

His mouth slightly open in astonishment, he nodded.

She laughed. Happiness and wonderment fluttered through her like a warm breeze. Up until this moment, being pregnant had been a concept, a fact but more of an idea than reality. Now, suddenly, everything became real. She wasn't pregnant as much as she was having a baby. *A child.* She was becoming a mom.

She blinked up at Marco. "That's our baby."

He stared at the screen as if dumbfounded. "Yeah."

She glanced at the doctor. "And he or she is fine?"

"From everything we can tell at this point, your baby is fine." He rose from his stool and took off his gloves. "Have you seen an obstetrician yet?"

"No. Actually, I haven't even chosen one."

He walked over to the sink to wash his hands. "I'll have the desk give you a list of recommendations." He picked up her chart and began making notes.

* * *

Marco could only stare at the screen. Connecting the image to the heartbeat made it all real. He was a father. He would play ball, make couch cushion forts, and teach a little someone how to brush his or her teeth.

The reality of the responsibility rolled over him but where it had overwhelmed him when Eleanora first told him, this time it sent a surge of strength through him. He had no clue if he could be a good dad, but he could research it. He *would* research it. He would not let his child grow up without a *good* father.

A ridiculous sense of pride surged through him, but just as quickly the responsibility came into sharp focus. He had been raised working in his family's hotels. His childhood was fun, but different. He didn't know what a normal childhood looked like, what a *good* dad did.

What if all the research in the world couldn't help him be a good father?

"You can get dressed now," the doctor said as he headed for the door. "Your paperwork will be at the front desk."

He left the room and Eleanora lifted herself to her elbows. "Why don't you wait outside while I redress?"

He glanced at her and realized she was naked under the sheet. He'd been so preoccupied with the potential that something might be wrong with her or the baby he hadn't even noticed. But with his attention drawn to the naked shoulders peeking out from the sheet, his mind whipped back to the images he had of her from their night together. Especially the smoothness of her pink skin.

"Earth to Marco. I'd like to get dressed and go home."

He shook himself back to reality. "Sorry. I'll be right outside the door if you need me."

She smiled patiently. "I'll be fine."

He stood in the hallway beside her small exam room until she came out. Together they gathered the discharge papers that included the names of some obstetricians. Outside the hospital, she turned to the left side of the parking lot.

He stopped her. "My car's this way."

"And my car's that way."

He gaped at her. "You drove yourself to the hospital!"

"Well, I wasn't going to call an ambulance when I felt okay—"

He rolled his eyes. "I'm following you home."

She sighed. "I wouldn't expect anything less."

He trailed her onto the main road to a neat little apartment complex not far from the Grand York Rome. She drove slowly and carefully through the noise and crowds of a city in the throes of its peak season. He suspected she did that to stem his fears—or potential criticism. She pulled into the parking lot with equal care, and he parked beside her.

Stuffing her discharge papers into her purse, she walked toward his car. "There. I'm home. Safe and sound."

The ambient sounds of the city surrounded them like the warm night air. "Why don't you let me walk you to your apartment?"

She sighed as if she knew arguing was point-less and motioned for him to follow her into the building. They climbed the stairway to her floor, and she led him into her apartment.

"This is nice." It reminded him of her. Tidy rooms with neutral toned furniture, but vivid-colored throw pillows and lamps that took the potentially dull rooms and made them bright and fun.

"You pay me enough to afford something nice."

He was glad they did. He took a few steps into the orderly but vibrant space. The kitchen with white cabinets was good-sized beside a dining area with a black table and gray upholstered chairs.

"Are you checking for intruders?"

He wasn't sure what he was doing but he sud-denly felt odd about leaving. "I don't know. It seems wrong to leave when you just came back from a hospital visit."

"Because I panicked. I'm new at this. I didn't know a little spotting was normal."

He shrugged. "Neither did I."

"That's why the very kind doctor did a scan."

He turned to face her. "It wasn't protocol?"

"No. He wanted to alleviate my fears. I could see him holding back a chuckle when you charged in. He knew we were new, and we needed some reassurance."

He thought back to the scan and swallowed hard. If he closed his eyes and focused, he could hear that heartbeat. The slow, solid sound that told him his child was fine.

"So, you're okay?"

She shrugged. "Perfectly."

"You don't want me to stay?"

She frowned and studied him for a second. "You want to stay, don't you?"

"I just had another whole set of feelings that threw me. I heard our baby's heartbeat. He or she might have been a little too small to see, but I heard that heartbeat."

"It was great, wasn't it?"

"Yes." He took a quick breath. "It would just make me feel better to stay here tonight."

She sighed.

"I'm not talking as the father of your child or

even your boss. I'm asking as your friend. I'm a little worried. Not big worried. Just a little worried. And you know how I hate things I can't control. Humor me. Let me stay." He paused, then added, "I'll sleep on the couch."

She laughed. "Well, at least I know you won't pull up a chair beside my bed and stare at me all night."

"I could. If you want me to."

She gaped at him. "No! Seriously! I'm fine." She shook her head. "But you're not. Okay. Whatever. Sleep on the couch." She turned to the bedroom door. "There are blankets and pillows in the linen closet in the hall. I'll see you in the morning."

"See you in the morning," he called after her. The relief of her letting him stay filled him, relaxing his chest and back. He didn't believe something was going to happen in the eight hours until morning, but he absolutely couldn't handle the thought of leaving her alone—just in case.

He made a bed out of the sofa and laughed to himself as he tried to get comfortable on a piece of furniture that was too small for his feet. He watched some television, careful to keep the sound low so he didn't wake her, and eventually fell asleep.

The ping of a text on his phone woke him.

He bounced up, and remembered he was on her couch at the same time that the scent of frying bacon hit him.

"Hey, good morning!" Her voice came from the kitchen in the corner of the open-plan space.

He sucked in a long breath trying to wake himself. "Good morning." He glanced down at his phone as he said that, tapping the screen to get to his text. Reading it, he frowned. "Pilot's ready for us."

She gaped at him. "What?"

"In fairness, I told him I wanted to leave first thing in the morning." He looked at the time on his phone screen and winced. "It's after nine."

She set the bacon on the countertop that divided the kitchen and sitting area. "I need to get dressed. Here's bacon. Eggs are in the refrigerator. Bread is on the counter to make toast."

With that she scampered away, and he texted his limo driver. He had to go back to the hotel to get his things and Eleanora probably needed to at least tell Sheila she would be in New York for a few days.

Knowing he had time to eat before the limo driver got there, he polished off the bacon with some toast and a cup of coffee, then he walked to the bedroom door.

Knocking once, he said, "Limo's here to pick me up. I need to go to the hotel to get my things.

You can come with me and have time to talk to Sheila or we can come back and pick you up."

She opened the door. Suitcase handle in one hand and wearing comfortable trousers and a white blouse, she smiled. "I'm ready when you are." She rolled the suitcase to the front door, indicating he should follow her. "I would like a minute to set up a few things with Sheila. But, seriously, with video calls the way they are, I can talk to my staff every day. It'll be like I'm there. They won't even miss me."

He smiled and nodded, but when she turned to lock the apartment door behind them, he swallowed. He'd seen her in white blouses and professional trousers a million times, so why they made his heart race this time he had no idea.

But he fully intended to get himself so accustomed to seeing her again that this attraction would wither away into nothing.

CHAPTER FOUR

THE SECOND THEY stepped off the private jet in New York, Eleanora smelled fall. It was the most beautiful season as far as she was concerned. The temperatures were mild, leaves turned from green to red and gold, then floated away in the November breezes, and the air smelled fresh and invigorating.

They entered the limo, and the driver took off without instruction. Marco usually texted his plans, so it didn't surprise her that he didn't tell his driver to take her to the Grand York before he took Marco to his penthouse.

She got comfortable on the seat, relaxing. The long plane ride had made her sleepy. Still on Italian time, her body believed it was almost seven o'clock at night. In Manhattan it was one in the afternoon. She knew she should stay up another nine hours to adjust to the time change, but a wave of tiredness swept over her. She'd read about the first trimester need to sleep and suspected that was kicking in.

Taking advantage of the short pause, she closed her eyes as Marco fiddled with his phone. She must have fallen asleep because it seemed like seconds before he was waking her.

"We're here."

She forced her eyes open. "Okay."

She exited the limo, expecting to be in the heart of the city, but the sidewalk was almost empty, the area quiet. As she glanced around, realizing they weren't at the Grand York, a doorman hustled out of the big white brick building.

He touched the rim of his cap. "Afternoon, ma'am." Grabbing the handle of her suitcase, then Marco's, he hurried inside.

"We're at your house?"

He shrugged. "We want privacy to figure this out, don't we?"

Still groggy from her nap, she thought it through. "Yeah. I guess."

"I *know*," he said, putting his hand on the small of her back to direct her into the lobby.

Walking through the ultramodern space with black metal light fixtures hanging from the high ceiling, simple red sofas flanked by glass tables and shiny marble floors, she wondered if Marco didn't have an ulterior motive in keeping her with him.

They'd barely spoken on the plane as each used their laptops to work through the seven-hour flight. But she knew the scare that had sent her to the hospital the night before had caused him to be overly protective. And it looked like he hadn't gotten over it.

They stepped into the private elevator and rode nonstop to the top floor, the penthouse. The doors opened on a floor plan that housed a kitchen, dining area and a living room with a wide-screen television over a stacked stone fireplace. In the far corner was a game area with pool and foosball tables, a dartboard on the wall and a wet bar.

Like the building lobby, all the furniture was sleek, black and white with chrome trim and legs on the tables. Beyond that was a floor-to-ceiling window with a view of Manhattan that almost made her head spin.

The place was gorgeous. Pristine. It was so different from his former condo, the one he'd bought before he was promoted into upper echelon management. That one had been comfy. This one dripped with wealth and privilege. It was so pretty she worried about sitting on the chairs.

The realization of how different they were rippled through her. They might have begun as what felt like equals when they'd met because of their fathers' friendship, but while her father had finished out his career and retired comfortably, Marco's dad had gone on to build an empire. She was simply an employee of that empire. Someday Marco and his sister would inherit everything that Marco and their father had built.

Two orange cats raced in from a long corridor that she assumed led to bedrooms. They wound themselves around Marco's ankles.

He stooped down to pet them. "Hey, dudes!"

"Hey, dudes?" She peered at him. "You have cats?"

"Eleanora, meet Sunrise and Sunset."

Still confused, she made a face at him. "You named your cats Sunrise and Sunset?"

"Well, look at them." He nudged his chin in the direction of the orange tabbies as he petted them. "Aren't they the color of a sunrise or a sunset?"

She frowned. "In what part of the world?"

"The Taj Mahal? The Isle of Skye in Scotland?"

As he easily recited places where he'd seen the sun rise and set, the uncomfortable feeling rolled through her again. He'd passed her career-wise and financially. While some people might say that shouldn't affect their friendship, how could it not? She traveled, but not like he could and obviously did. She could never afford a penthouse in a building like this with a doorman.

He laughed as he rose. "We've got to work on getting you to relax." He headed for the kitchen. "But right now, everybody gets a treat."

He ambled toward the cabinets. The cats gracefully trotted behind him. Two gorgeous tabbies with sleek fur and fluffy tails, they were probably the prettiest cats she'd ever seen.

He retrieved a bag from one of the white cabinets and she noticed the pearly gray backsplash that pulled gray tones from the marble countertops.

Using both hands, he set two piles of bite-sized treats on the floor, a small stack for each cat, spaced an arm's distance apart.

He glanced up at Eleanora. "To avoid fighting."

She laughed. "Seriously?"

"Have you never owned a cat?"

"I personally haven't. No."

"Did you parents have a cat?"

She shook her head.

He rose from his stooped position by the cats. "So much to teach you."

He sounded like the Marco she knew, but though he was teasing, that strange feeling tumbled through her again. Except this time, it wasn't about how different Marco was. This time, being in his penthouse mixed with his sudden desire to get back to New York, and she wondered if he didn't have plans he wasn't sharing.

Testing that theory, she carefully said, "I'm only going to be here a few days. No need to get all fussy about teaching me."

As the elevator door opened again and the doorman entered with their luggage, Marco said, "It's optimistic to think we only need a few days. We could spend a month figuring out everything we have to discuss."

A month?

Marco faced the doorman. "Good afternoon, Arnie."

"Afternoon, sir." Arnie rolled their luggage a few feet in front of the elevator, tipped his hat and was gone in seconds.

Eleanora felt like a deer in the headlights, as Marco easily, happily directed her down the hall.

"This is your room," he said, opening the door onto a lovely, spa-like space. Pale brown wood floors were protected by a huge handwoven white area rug. A dove-gray bedspread accented the multi-wood headboard. Lamps with drum shades and aqua bases matched the aqua and white drapes. A coral-colored pillow gave it a pop of whimsy.

She pulled her suitcase inside. Mixed feelings or not, she loved this space. "This room is lovely!"

"Thank you. But I can't take any credit. I hired a decorator."

Of course he had. Her weird feelings returned as another piece of the Marco she knew fell away.

He took a step to the right and opened a door with a light tap. "Your bathroom."

She smiled and nodded at the aqua, white and gray bathroom. Stunning and spa-like, it was nothing like what the old Marco had in his former condo.

"Now, let's both change into something comfortable because I'm guessing Sunrise and Sunset want a walk."

She snapped out of her worry that something more was going on here and peeked at him. "A walk? You walk your cats?"

"Yeah. They love a good walk. I'm sure the pet sitter took them out this morning, but I'm also guessing they missed me. And after all those hours of sitting on the flight and the drive here, I wouldn't mind stretching my legs. I'm sure you could use a walk too." He headed for the door but turned back again. "Jeans are good."

He left and she opened her suitcase. She pulled out her favorite jeans and it hit her again that soon she wouldn't be able to wear any of the clothes she loved—

The craziness of her situation froze her.

She was in New York instead of Rome.

She'd soon swell up and pee when she laughed.

Because she and someone she considered her *best friend* were going to have a baby together.

And Marco was Marco but not the same.

She'd thought her life had changed when she read the pregnancy test. But this right here? Being swept off to New York? Seeing differences in Marco? Walking cats? Her world felt like it had flipped upside down. She'd thought Marco would accept the fact that she was pregnant, but distance himself. She kind of pictured herself going through pregnancy alone.

And childbirth.

And raising their son or daughter with only sporadic visits from Marco—who, let's face it, was extremely busy with his job.

But he'd flown her to New York, slid her into his house and soon would have her walking his cats with him—technically sucking her into his world.

She slipped into her jeans. The truth she'd been avoiding couldn't be ignored anymore. No matter how much her inner planner wished it, this situation wasn't going to be easy. It was going to get complicated. Because Marco was a more obsessive planner than she was. Worse, he was also accustomed to getting his own way.

She had to stop him before he made radical plans like move her to New York—

As her boss, he could take away the managership of the Grand York Rome and put her in the corporate office!

No.

She had to get control of this now. They had to start talking *now*. The longer she waited the more she risked that he would decide to keep her in New York.

What better time to start the discussions than while he was unwinding walking his cats?

Thinking of walking cats made her laugh and shake her head. But, hey. If he wanted to walk his cats? Fine. No matter how silly, it was an opportunity to get the ball rolling on the discussions they had to have.

Though sunny, it was a chilly November afternoon. She pulled a thick sweater over her T-shirt and grabbed her sunglasses from her purse. Returning to the front room, she found Marco and Sunrise and Sunset waiting for her by the elevator. While the cats were decked out in harnesses attached to leashes, he wore jeans and a fisherman's knit sweater. Ordinary clothes. But on him? Wow.

She swallowed hard. Keeping control of her life was reason number one to immediately begin the discussions they needed to have about their baby. But the attraction she felt to him was reason number two. He was so damned good-looking and so physically fit. She needed to get the hell back to Rome so she could stop going breathless when doing ordinary things like seeing him in a sweater and nice-fitting jeans.

Especially since he didn't seem to be fighting the same attraction to her.

When they reached the quiet street, she said the first thing that came to mind. "I thought you'd be a dog person?"

He laughed as Sunrise and Sunset trotted along in front of them. They didn't sniff like dogs or pause for potty breaks. It almost seemed the two tabbies were people watching.

"No. I'm a cat person. My mom had a German Shepherd that drove me crazy. Though I like a pet, I went for a simpler animal. Cats aren't as needy."

She laughed. "Yet you walk your cats. I think you liked some stuff about owning a dog."

"I guess."

"So—" She gave him a second to glance at her. "Where do we start?"

"Where do we start about what?"

"We need to discuss the elephant in the room."

"There are so many elephants in our room, I'm not sure which one you're talking about."

She almost suggested they start their baby

discussions with his thoughts on visitation but realized that was something a couple worked up to. She considered asking how he thought raising a child together would work when she lived on one continent and he lived on another, but that took them right back to visitation and she'd already nixed that.

Besides, the most obvious elephant in their room was their living arrangements. She and Marco weren't people who played games. They discussed things openly. But he hadn't mentioned bringing her to his penthouse.

"Okay, let's start with this. Why did you bring me to your house instead of letting me stay at the hotel?"

He didn't even hesitate. "I told you. Privacy."

A few snowflakes fluttered around them. Given the cold, Eleanora wasn't surprised. But she wished she'd brought a jacket. Her thick sweater might be warm but the early November sun was deceptive.

"Not only will we have more time to talk things out, but also there's no worry about anyone overhearing."

"But I have work—"

"Which you can do from the penthouse." A look of comprehension suddenly lit his face. "You want time away from me." He shook his head. "That's easily handled. I can set you up in the corporate office."

She blinked. Giving her a place in the corporate office was the first step to installing her there permanently. She'd walked right into that! But she could also fix it.

"With virtual meetings and video calling I can work from the penthouse, thanks. I'm just surprised you think it's going to take us so long to make our decisions."

He cut her a look. "I'm surprised you don't."

The wind picked up. The snowflakes grew in number. She shivered.

"Come on. Let's get you back." Shifting the leashes to his right hand, he slid his left arm across her shoulders and nestled her against his side to warm her.

The sweetness of the gesture and soft tone of his voice shot her back to their night together. Making love had been so simple, so effortless for them that she had been sure they'd started something. With his arm around her, she wished they had. She wished she could snuggle against his warm fisherman's sweater, wished they'd go back to his apartment and set a fire in the beautiful fireplace and make love in front of it.

Maybe rebelling against staying at his penthouse was wrong? Their night together had been so wonderful that spending more time together might be what they needed. Laughing, talking things out, might get him past his doubts and regrets. Living together might show him what she'd felt the night they'd made love. That they were made for each other.

She shook her head to clear it.

Really? Was that actually what she believed? Or was she wishful thinking?

They'd had their shot at shifting from friends to lovers and he hadn't wanted it. She must have been a letdown as a lover for him to stay away from her as he had the week after the grand opening, and then to succinctly tell her that what they'd started wouldn't go on.

Not *couldn't* go on—as if there was a choice. *Wouldn't* go on—as if he'd made an irrevocable decision.

Bringing her to New York, being concerned about her, even drawing her to his side to keep her warm, was only for their baby.

Marco's voice broke into her thoughts. "The decisions we have to make are about more than child support, custody or even visitation. Right now, those might seem like the most important things. But they aren't. We are about to *raise a child*. There are so many things about childrearing that we don't know. I've never envisioned being a father so I'm starting at square one. You were raised by normal parents. You might be okay. But my dad was always working—traveling to look for new spots to expand. When I got old enough, he gave me little jobs at the hotel—but I felt like I had to grow up from that day on. Then my mom got sick, and our family totally changed. I've never envisioned being a father, so all this is new to me. I'm sure I have a boatload of wrong beliefs about raising kids."

"I'm sure you do." She knew that because she'd watched him grow up. The differences in their worlds and their ways of thinking were beginning to show up now, proving his fears about raising a child together weren't unfounded. Worse, those differences also pointed out that they did not belong together. There'd be no more daydreaming or wishful thinking. She couldn't afford the risk. Not when her child's future was at stake. And her friendship with Marco. If their discussions brought out disagreements that turned into fights, their friendship could be over.

She tried to imagine her life without Marco. Without his wit and wisdom. His charm. The way he listened when she talked. The way he pushed her to be her best.

The emptiness that shuddered through her soul was almost unbearable.

He might not want her as a lover, but they

were good friends. They shared history and experiences.

She did not want to lose him.

Before they made it back to Marco's building, the snowflakes had all but disappeared and the sun came out from behind a cloud, warming the air a bit. Eleanora slid herself out from under his arm and shifted away from him.

He wasn't sure if he should be happy or disappointed. The strangest feeling had risen when he'd put his arm around her, a click of rightness that he'd first thought related to their friendship. But he'd realized the only other time he'd felt it was at the grand opening celebration. That click caused him to open a door that he should have left closed. He allowed the feeling to take him back to that night and everything he'd felt. The breathless anticipation as he'd undressed her. The bliss of feeling her skin brush his. The thunderbolts of need when they'd kissed.

It was insanity to let himself remember and she'd reminded him of that when she'd shifted away as soon as the sun provided a wisp of warmth.

Because they were friends who'd made a mistake when they'd crossed the line and slept together.

Arnie greeted them as they walked Sunrise

and Sunset to the elevator. Neither said a word on the ride up to the penthouse.

After removing the cat harnesses, he suggested a fire. She'd shrugged and said she wanted to shower before dinner. Suddenly he was alone with the cats, who sat in front of him like sentries, poised in anticipation.

"Red light?" he asked.

They perked up. He found the laser light in a drawer and watched them run around chasing it.

This was his life. A single guy with the best job in the world who was making his family wealthy. He had cats for company because dogs were more work. And he dated. He had relationships. He simply would never marry, never commit long term. Not just because relationships ended. Because he was too busy.

More than that, he was happy. He'd chosen this life. Circumstances in his past had informed that decision. The loss of his mom. Needing to help his dad take the business to the next level. But most people didn't get opportunities like his. He would never forget that.

His brain whispered that sleeping with Eleanora had been an opportunity too. But he shut it down. Eleanora was a woman who believed in happily-ever-after. She'd never find it with a guy more committed to his family's business than her. She wanted moonlight walks and kisses in the rain. He was not that guy.

What might have been an interesting opportunity for him was a dead end for her.

He liked her too much to forget that.

CHAPTER FIVE

ELEANORA FELT BETTER as she warmed herself in the steam of the hot shower, but she was not happy that they hadn't really discussed their situation. If anything, his suggestion that she could work from the corporate office made her believe he was veering them off in a direction that would cost her the job she'd worked so hard to get.

She dressed in sweats and an oversize T-shirt, more convinced than ever that she had to get away from him before he'd subtly guided her back to Manhattan. She agreed that her staying in the penthouse gave them private time to talk things through. But that meant they had to start talking. Otherwise, she'd be here forever, making her situation worse because doing things together only reminded her of why she liked him. She needed to get rid of those feelings so they could return to their normal friendship. If they couldn't, he'd be right. Their night together would have ruined a very happy friendship that stretched the whole way back to their childhood.

Neither one of them wanted to lose that.

Her determination restored, she entered the front room at the same time the elevator doors opened, and a gorgeous woman stepped inside. About twenty-five, with big blue pixie eyes, wearing yoga pants and cute boots, she unzipped her winter coat. With a hood trimmed in fur, the sexy little jacket made her look like a ski bunny. Her broad smile warmed the room.

Marco raced to the elevator. "I'm so sorry! I forgot to text to let you know I'd come home early."

She smiled beatifically. "That's okay."

The cats appeared out of nowhere. Like crazed males, they raced to the pretty girl and wound around her ankles. She stooped down to pet them.

"Hello, gentlemen."

As if finally realizing she was there, Marco glanced at Eleanora. "Oh, Eleanora, this is Wisdom…my pet sitter."

Eleanora stifled a groan. She even had one of those ethereal names that all beautiful women had. "It's nice to meet you."

"Wisdom, this is my friend, Eleanora."

Still stooped in front of the cats, happy Wisdom smiled. "Nice to meet you too." She looked up at Marco, as the cats rubbed up against her and purred as she petted them. "So, you're back?"

"Yes. Probably for a whole month. I'll pay you for the two weeks I was supposed to be gone."

Wisdom nodded, rose and pressed the elevator button to open the door again. "Okay. Call when you need me."

Eleanora knew she was talking about Marco calling for pet sitting services, but Eleanora's vivid imagination took that all wrong. The doors opened and the pet sitter got in and waved goodbye to the cats, then disappeared behind the closing doors.

"I feel like an idiot for forgetting to text her, making her come here when she didn't need to."

Eleanora settled into the sofa, feet tucked beneath her bottom, trying not to be jealous. "She didn't seem to mind."

Marco ambled over. "Yeah. She's a good person."

Eleanora glanced right, then left. There wasn't a thing around her to pretend interest in, so she could feign indifference. Unless she wanted to fixate on a lamp, she had no recourse but to look at him. "Cats seemed to like her."

He laughed. "Of course they do. She feeds them. And speaking of food, are you ready for dinner? We can order just about anything you want and have it here in an hour."

"An hour?" Her stomach picked that precise second to growl.

He laughed. "It's good to see you get hungry. How about this? I always have things in the refrigerator. Cheese. Deli meat. Stuff for salad."

"Got any bread?"

He nodded.

She rose from the sofa. "I can make us toasted cheese sandwiches."

He motioned her back down again. "No. This is my house. I'm host. You can turn on the TV or pick a book." He pointed to a low bookcase along a back wall that she hadn't noticed. "I'll have sandwiches ready in ten minutes."

She slowly sat again. She wasn't in the mood for television or a book, but she wasn't going to argue with him about her being in one room while he was in another. The fire he'd set created a warm, cozy feeling that seemed to be intensifying her romantic feelings for him. Even her jealousy over gorgeous Wisdom disappeared in a wave of happiness at being alone with him.

She squeezed her eyes shut. She either had to get rid of these feelings, or she and Marco had to get down to business with their discussions so she could go home.

Marco left the living area and walked to the kitchen where he began to prepare their simple

dinner. He loved the fact that Eleanora so easily got comfortable in the penthouse, but her
behavior was still off—

And she'd made that comment about Wisdom.

He thought that through as he gathered bread,
cheese and butter and two cans of tomato soup
his housekeeper had stocked just in case. Today
was a just-in-case day if he ever saw one. His
hormones were popping around a woman he'd
always considered a friend and she'd reacted
oddly about Wisdom.

He didn't like to speculate but he seriously
wondered if she had been jealous.

He almost laughed at the idea of gorgeous,
successful Eleanora being jealous of anyone—
except things had changed between them since
they'd slept together. She might not want to be
jealous, but her hormones—like his—might be
pulling more strings than she let on.

He rolled the idea around in his head as he
buttered bread and set it sizzling into a frying
pan before covering it with cheese and topping
it with another slice of buttered bread.

What if she was jealous?

He laughed with delight at the possibility, as
a much-needed boost of pride surged through
him. That would mean she wasn't as unaffected
by their night together as she continually led
him to believe.

He finished the sandwiches, heated the soup and set everything out on the table before calling her to dinner.

She sluggishly sat on one of the chairs at the round table. He swore he could see a dark cloud over her head. Something obviously bothered her. It didn't take a genius to realize she could have been thinking about the pregnancy, custody and visitation discussions ahead of them. She might have even been thinking about her job.

Unless she really had been jealous of Wisdom?

She gave him a weak smile. "I'm sorry I left dinner to you, but the plane ride really seemed to take something out of me. Plus, I'm still on Italy time. Technically, I should be going to bed right now."

He sat beside her. Being tired might have made her unable to hide her feelings about Wisdom—which, now that he took a minute to think it through—really meant she had feelings for *him*. "And you're pregnant. I understand tiredness is one of the complications of the first trimester."

She sighed. "I forgot how much you like to research."

"It always helps to know what you're dealing with."

For the first time since she'd told him she was pregnant, the scales felt balanced. Being attracted to each other was a problem, but it was a better problem than believing he was the only one who was suffering. He supposed misery really did love company, or in this case misery made them even, putting them on a level playing field.

With that rationalization making him feel better, he could hold a normal conversation with her. But about what? What didn't slide up against their attraction—which neither one of them would want to discuss? Even her pregnancy related back to sleeping together so that had to be out. Plus, discussing her pregnancy brought its own problems. Like living on two different continents. Would he have to fly to Rome every time it was his turn to have the baby? And what about child support? He could pay her a small fortune, enough that she wouldn't have to work if she didn't want to. But would that insult her? Would it make her feel he was easing her out of her job because she had a baby?

That was a lawsuit waiting to happen. Everything else was a potential fight. They needed a little more time to chill and get comfortable with each other before they faced some of their thorny issues.

"I know a way to perk you up." He reached for his sandwich. "We never did fully discuss your hotel's numbers yesterday. What do I need to know?"

"Wouldn't it be better to start sorting through some of the baby stuff?"

He'd already decided that was still too risky of a subject. "Let's save that for when you have a little more energy. Hit me with your numbers."

With a belabored sigh, she launched into a report of the hotel's progress. They had both been in the industry long enough they had a short-hand of a sort that made the discussion easy—a lot less complicated than trying to decide who'd get their baby when and what kind of child support he would provide.

"Those numbers are amazing."

"I think Rome was just ready for the type of hotel we built." She ate a bite of sandwich.

"Upscale?"

"Yes. Upscale but comfortable. A resort in the middle of the city."

He took a spoonful of soup. Though from a can, it was delicious on the cold night.

She gave her reasoning behind the hotel's success, not just advertising but word of mouth, connections with travel professionals and how she made them work in her favor. By the time she was done, they were finished eating. Color had also come back to her cheeks. She appeared to have energy.

"You look better. I think you just needed to eat."

She laughed. "Maybe."

He smiled at her. She smiled back at him. Their normal feelings for each other seemed to return. But he couldn't forget his suspicion that she might have been jealous about Wisdom. God help him, he was smart enough to recognize that only made their problem worse. But his male pride had taken such a beating over how easily she accepted his decision to remain friends that he didn't think his private recognition of their attraction was out of line. He'd just keep the conversation on work, and they'd be fine.

"Talking to you about your job is always easy. You don't hide anything like some of our other managers, so there's no pulling teeth."

She shrugged. "You're the same way. Always up front with me." She stopped. Her forehead wrinkled as she frowned.

He frowned too. Was she rethinking that compliment because she believed there was something between him and Wisdom? Something he was keeping secret?

That wasn't good. If they really were going to be fair with each other about raising their child, she had to know he wasn't keeping secrets.

"There's nothing going on between me and Wisdom."

She blinked. "What?"

"Well, you just seemed to have an odd reaction to her—"

"Odd reaction?"

He didn't want to say the word *jealousy.* "You know. You're usually chipper when you meet new people. Even women—"

"Even *women*?"

She would not let him finish a sentence and that was bad. Very bad. If he said the word *jealousy* right now, she'd probably pop him.

Her eyes widened. "Oh, I get it. You thought I was jealous."

There wasn't a snowball's chance in hell that he'd admit that.

Too much time passed. Her face reddened, then she rose and began gathering their dishes and soup bowls. "Let's clear the table."

He cursed in his head. He'd certainly screwed that up and there wasn't even a wisp of an idea in his frozen brain for how to fix it. He grabbed their glasses and followed her into the kitchen and set them by the sink.

She rinsed the bowls and stacked them in the dishwasher. He stood behind her, so confused he didn't know what to do. But one thought did pop into his befuddled brain. If she hadn't been at least a bit jealous, she'd have ribbed him about being wrong. Instead, she said nothing...

And continued to say nothing.

There was definitely something there.

She turned to walk away from the sink before he had sufficient time to shift away and suddenly they were face-to-face, two inches away from each other. If he moved forward a fragment of a step or she edged up a bit, they'd be touching.

Just thinking about touching her sent his nerve endings into a spasm. The pull of his need to make things right coupled with his attraction to her. They latched onto him and wouldn't let go. He swore he could feel himself being sucked toward her as if she were a magnet.

She didn't move. He didn't even think she was breathing. With their gazes locked, he let his body inch ever closer to her. He should be fighting this, but he couldn't seem to combat instincts so strong his muscles quivered from the effort.

When she didn't protest or move away, he saw the longing in her eyes. Not anger. Longing.

Relief poured through him, and he realized they needed this moment of pure honesty. They weren't the kind of people who were supposed to be at odds, fighting an attraction, hesitating about how they would raise a child together. They were meant to click. To be good to each other. To like each other.

Their mouths met slowly, cautiously. The touch of their lips became a reverent acknowledgment of how special this was. But the sweet relief quickly morphed into need. He caught her upper arms and eased her closer. She melted against him.

The kiss shifted into a frenzy of desperation. One minute they were fighting the longing that arched between them. The next they had given in, and the pleasure of kissing her made him even hungrier for everything they'd had the night of the grand opening.

He stopped thinking. He refused to consider the ramifications and simply enjoyed the softness of her lips, the warm ridges of her tongue, as desperation gave way to aggression, and he took what he wanted.

Then suddenly she was gone. His eyes popped open to see she was by the kitchen island, as if she'd jumped back, getting as far away from him as she could in one frantic move.

For a second, they stared at each other. The consequences he'd chosen to ignore bounced into his head. Kissing confused their relationship.

In twenty-odd years of friendship, they'd never kissed. Now they hadn't merely had an ill-advised night together; they'd kissed. They hadn't just crossed the line once; they'd crossed it again.

Or he'd crossed it.

Something that looked a lot like disappointment filled her eyes.

She turned and walked toward the hall that led to the bedrooms. "I'm exhausted. I'll see you in the morning."

He watched her go, his mouth falling open in confusion. He'd seen longing in her eyes. He'd sworn she'd been jealous of Wisdom.

Yet she was disappointed in him?

Was this what had happened the night of the grand opening? Had he misinterpreted that night, too?

Memories from their night together crowded his mind. Kissing her had happened naturally then too, and he'd had enough champagne to let himself go and enjoy. Still, she'd been right with him, as happy as he was.

Then after that ill-fated night, they'd talked about not getting romantically involved—

No. *He'd* been the one to suggest it. Actually, he'd more or less *demanded* it.

Then he'd kissed her again?

No wonder she was disappointed in him. He'd broken his own rule.

He shook his head as he bent down to stroke Sunset's fluffy fur.

He had to fix this.

CHAPTER SIX

AFTER SHOWERING AND dressing for work the next morning, Eleanora took a long, slow breath and walked to the kitchen area where Marco stood by the center island, pulling take-out containers from a plastic bag. Sunrise and Sunset sat on the sofa in the living room, grooming themselves, obviously having already eaten.

"What's this?"

"Breakfast takeout. I called in the order, and they had it here within ten minutes." He nudged his chin in the direction of the round table. "If we hurry and eat, our eggs won't be cold."

Her stomach quietly rumbled. Not one to punish herself by pretending she wasn't hungry so she could avoid him, she reached for one of the take-out containers. She'd leave the conversation up to Mr. I-Don't-Want-to-Have-a-Relationship-with-You. The same guy who'd kissed her.

She damn well hoped he had an explanation for kissing her because he could not have it both ways. She'd been halfway in love with him most of her life. She'd thought she'd gotten her big shot with him the night of the grand opening celebration, but he was sorry they'd slept together.

He shouldn't be kissing her.

She ignored the little voice that reminded her that she shouldn't have enjoyed it, though her breath stuttered at the memory. But she straightened her shoulders. There would have been nothing to enjoy if he hadn't made the first move.

"Want a plate?"

She headed for the table. "No. I can eat out of the box. I want to get into the office."

He frowned and grabbed silverware from a drawer. "You do?" At the table, he handed her a fork, knife and spoon. "I thought you were going to work from here?"

"Mostly. But this morning I want to call Rome and talk to the restaurant manager." Keeping her eyes and hands busy with her takeout, she added, "There are some things I'd like him to try."

She sat, opened her container and found a cheese omelet, dry rye toast and bacon. The scent of it drifted to her and her stomach growled again. She dug in.

He didn't ask her what things she wanted her restaurant manager to try. Devoted to ensuring his hotels were the best in the world, Marco usually wanted to know every detail. Which meant he was hesitating because of that kiss.

Or it could mean he regretted their kiss and wanted to pretend it hadn't happened. If that was the case, she swore she would lambaste him.

She took another two bites of omelet. Silence sat heavily over the table.

Finally, he said, "Aren't we going to talk about what happened last night?"

Irritation jangled through her. She set her fork on the table. "What happened last night? Don't you mean what *you did* last night?" If he gave her the let's-pretend-it-didn't-happen sermon again, she seriously would throttle him.

"Honestly, I felt something and let myself go." He took a breath. "I'm sorry. I'm the guy who doesn't want anything to happen between us and I broke that trust."

His food on a plate, he sat on the chair beside her, forcing her to give him her full attention. "Listen to me. The reason I don't want anything to happen between us involves me. Not you. You are wonderful. You are smart. You are beautiful and you are so soft the temptation to touch you really is hard to resist."

She swallowed, listening to the kinds of beautiful words she'd always wanted to hear from him, knowing from his tone that a *but* was coming.

"But I'm not the kind of person to settle down.

Everyone believes that when the perfect partner comes along, you'll forget your past and your reasons for framing your life the way you did. But it's not true or you would have made me forget every one of my reasons after our night together. Instead, I woke up with them pounding in my head. My dad lost everything when he lost my mom. He became so driven he didn't have time to think about his loss and could fall into bed exhausted at night. I would watch him and think that was no way to live."

What he saw as awful, she saw as beautiful. Joshua loved his wife so much he pined for her when she was gone. "Maybe that's because your parents had a once-in-a-lifetime love?"

"And you're saying it would be different for us? That we *wouldn't* have a once-in-a-lifetime-love?"

Her heart stuttered at the thought that what they had was common, ordinary.

He took her hand. "You *want* a once-in-a-life-time-love. I've known it since we were kids. But I don't. I've seen the other side. I've seen the hurt and the pain. I could never be all in. I'd always hold a piece of myself back and work would provide every opportunity to do that." He stopped long enough to connect his gaze with hers. "I don't want to hurt you."

Whatever he felt for her, it was strong. She

could see it in his eyes. He would never in good conscience hurt her. He hadn't run away the morning after their tryst because she wasn't good enough but because what they'd had that night had tempted him enough that he saw the trouble ahead.

Not giving her a chance to speak, he rose from the table. "I won't kiss you again. I won't slip up again. Now that we're on the same page, now that you understand, I'm pretty sure we'll be okay."

Overwhelmed by his sincerity, she pressed her lips together and nodded.

He started to walk away but stopped suddenly and faced her again. "To be clear... I'm not going to treat you differently because you're pregnant with my child. I'm not going to take away your job or transfer you to the corporate office so we can all be in Manhattan. But we do have to talk logically and honestly about how we can raise a child together when we live on two different continents. And I don't think we're going to be able to force it. I think the conversation will have to happen naturally, after we've both had time to think about it—and have figured out what we want. That way we'll have a starting point for compromise."

He headed back down the hall. When he returned to the main room, he was shrugging into his suit coat. "Want to ride to work with me?"

"Aren't you going to eat?"

He grabbed his briefcase from beside the kitchen island. "Not as hungry as I thought I was."

"Okay. But I want to eat. Then I have to dress and gather my things."

"Take all the time you need. I'll send the limo back for you."

Because that was something normal Marco would suggest, she nodded. He left.

Sunrise and Sunset sent her condemning looks from their seats on the sofa.

"What? That wasn't really a fight. Plus, he started it." She took a breath. "And he finished it. With logic. And reasoning." She shook her head. "Damn it. I understand. I was around for his mother's death. Joshua melted." She paused for a few seconds. "And Marco's a wealthy, busy guy whose love is his family's legacy. Of course, he's not going to put a hundred percent into a relationship. I get it. Even if we married, I'd be like a trophy wife." She frowned. "Not a trophy, more like a dutiful wife." The hair on the back of her neck rose. No smart woman wanted that. At home with the kids, planning weekend barbecues and dinner parties while he traveled the globe, hobnobbing with jet-setters as he ran the family business. "He'd give me enough attention that I'd be okay… But he'd never be mine. He'll never be anybody's."

With that realization, her personal sadness morphed into acceptance of a sort. *That was his point.* He never would be anybody's. Not completely.

The cats lost interest. Sunset, the cat with a little more brown on his ears, settled in for a nap. Sunrise jumped off the sofa and trotted to the wall of windows. He found a spot on the floor warmed by the sun's rays, rolled himself into a ball and fell asleep.

Eleanora finished her breakfast. Sam texted that he was on his way, and she scrambled to clean up and get ready for work. By the time he pulled into the space in front of Marco's building, she was on the sidewalk waiting.

At his big mahogany desk, Marco kept his head down and worked through the morning, feeling the best he had since the grand opening. He should have given Eleanora the complete explanation of why he didn't want a romance with her the day he'd called her to tell her he only wanted to be friends. Instead, he'd told her that as boss and employee they shouldn't have a relationship. He'd also reminded her that he didn't want to lose their friendship when their romance inevitably ended.

This morning the whole truth had come out naturally because they really were friends, and she really did know him and his life. There was no reason for secrecy or partial reasoning. She could understand the truth.

The only problem was he hadn't given her a chance to speak. He'd wanted everything he'd said to sink in. He'd said his piece and left, giving her time alone in the penthouse to come to her own conclusions.

He didn't really know if she accepted what he'd said. Oh, he knew she understood it, but whether she accepted it was another story.

His assistant, Timothy, alerted him when she'd arrived. The office manager had been instructed to put her in an empty office at the back of the floor and he assumed she was there. He waited an hour for her to make her call with her Italian staff, then waited another five minutes before he ambled to the office she was using.

Standing in the doorway, he said, "Are we okay?"

She sat back. "Yes."

The expression on her face showed caution, but her eyes were sincere.

"Good." He waited a beat. "Want to go to lunch?"

"No. I'm fine." She smiled. "Big breakfast."

He chuckled. "Okay." He turned to go but she stopped him.

"Marco?"

He faced her again.

"I do understand."

Realizing she wanted the chance to have her say, he walked back into her office. "Really?"

"Yes, and there's a part of me that's grateful that you reminded me of some things." She laughed. "You know how I don't want you badgering me about eating?"

He was aware. "Yes."

"Your situation is a little different, but it's sort of the same. You are who you are. You've made choices and decisions. I know you like your life. I wouldn't want to change you."

Grateful she really did understand, he nodded.

"But I won't say I'm sorry we're having a child together. It's going to be weird, but if any two people can figure this out, it's us."

Relief swamped him. "Agreed."

"So go get lunch and let me get back to work."

"Okay."

He left and she sat staring at the door. Disappointment that they'd never be more than friends tried to form, but she squelched it. Of all the breakups she'd had—and whether Marco liked it or not their decision to be friends did feel like a breakup of a sort—this one had been the cleanest and maybe the wisest. Loss of her teenage boyfriend had devastated her. Loss of her first real lover had been odd. The relationship felt so permanent that when it ended, she almost couldn't wrap her head around it. But the clincher was her last boyfriend. She'd made a fool of herself with Quincy. He wooed her into believing he loved her when all he wanted was a connection to Joshua so he could get an introduction to the guy who owned the Grand York hotels. When Quincy had spent enough time with Joshua that Marco's dad knew who he was and that his company could become a Grand York supplier, he dropped her like yesterday's garbage.

The insult of that rattled through her. The humiliation of being such an easy mark had followed her for years. So much so that she'd begun keeping all her relationships casual. Sure, she dated but no one would ever fool her again.

She shook her head to rid it of the embarrassment. But her mind unexpectedly cleared. In the years since Quincy, no one *had* fooled her. That humiliation had made her stronger, smarter.

The truth of her life came into a little bit more focus, especially when she considered it against everything Marco had told her that morning about his choices. Seeing her life through that lens, seeing what she had, who she wanted to be, how she'd met so many of her goals, she sat back in her chair. She was thirty-one now, succeeding professionally and extremely happy living abroad. In Italy for Pete's sake! How lucky was that?

She suddenly wondered why she wanted to get married. Even Marco saw she wanted the once-in-a-lifetime love. But why?

Technically, she had everything. A great job. A great condo. She lived in Italy and her chances for promotions to places like Paris and London were high, given the Grand York's desire to expand. If she'd ever worried about her biological clock, she need worry no more. She was pregnant. This child would make her a mom.

What did she think she was going to get in a once-in-a-lifetime love?

What even made her believe a once-in-a-lifetime love was possible?

Even Joshua's perfect, once-in-a-lifetime love had ended in tragedy.

What if Marco was right? What if there was no such thing as the fairytale?

An unexpected curiosity filled her. What would it be like to just enjoy her life? Not tinker with perfection, but simply enjoy what she had without spoiling it with thoughts of tomorrow and a guy who may or may not exist?

It would probably be bliss. At the very least, she'd live in the moment, not miss a second of this wonderful career and all her opportunities.

Her computer buzzed with another conference call from her head of housekeeping. She straightened in her seat. This was what she loved. It was time she began enjoying it.

She worked through everyone's lunch hour. When the corporate office's support staff and accountants began to return, her staff in Rome was heading home.

Marco stopped in her doorway. "When you're ready, I would like to talk about the corporation's five-year plan and where the Rome hotel fits in the grand scheme of things."

She glanced up. "Okay."

"My office."

"Okay." With the feeling of normalcy restored, and her new curiosity about enjoying what she had capturing her imagination, she smiled. "I'll be there in a minute."

"See you then."

He left and she took a happy breath. She knew the honest conversation with Marco had gone a long way to restore harmony between them, but she felt lighter somehow. As if a great weight had been lifted.

And maybe it had?

In deciding not to worry or wonder about a long-term relationship or searching for the man of her dreams, she'd literally given herself permission to be happy with who she was.

She grabbed a notebook and some pens from her desk and headed to Marco's office.

He spent two hours going over the company's five-year plan with her, highlighting the Grand York Rome's position and how it could impact future growth in Europe.

She took it all in, but with a fresh perspective. At the right moment, she said, "Have you ever considered making me the manager of all new hotels in Europe?"

He set his pencil down and peered at her. "You want to manage eight or ten hotels?"

"No. I want to transfer to each new hotel to help build it, staff it, open it."

"I thought you liked Rome."

"I do! But wouldn't it be interesting and fun for me to do a little globetrotting?"

He carefully said, "You'll have a child."

"And you won't even begin serious planning on the Paris hotel for a year. By the time it would be necessary for me to move, our baby will be born, and I'll have a routine established. By the time Grand York moves on to the London project, our baby will be five or so. I'll have a great nanny. I won't settle for less than a great nanny. Our baby and I will be fine."

CHAPTER SEVEN

MARCO COULDN'T STOP thinking about her suggestion that afternoon. He understood Eleanora's desire to be a sort of traveling manager, setting up new hotels, getting them running smoothly and then moving on to the next beautiful European setting.

He understood what she was saying about their baby's life not really being impacted by moves—at least not until he or she got into school.

But he did not like the idea of having her set up every hotel and then walking away. There'd be no sense of continuity or consistency for the hotel or its staff.

Worse, he'd promised her that her pregnancy or motherhood wouldn't impede her position at work, then she asked for a major promotion?

He told himself not to obsess about that. He told himself that Eleanora was a trustworthy employee who wouldn't take advantage of him and forced down the nagging sensation that kept telling him there was more to this than met the eye.

Added to his odd feelings about her asking for a promotion right after he'd told her that her pregnancy wouldn't affect her job, he now wondered about her bringing up the idea of a new position when there were other things they had to decide.

He might have suggested they wait for the right time, but he genuinely believed her concerns about her pregnancy and their child should trump her wanting a promotion.

His business sense screamed there was something off in her suggestion but thinking she was using him didn't fit with his personal knowledge of her.

Still confused at the end of the day, he watched out the window behind Eleanora's desk, as he waited for her to gather her things to return to the penthouse. They were back to being friends. But he couldn't stop the nagging sense that he was missing something.

He knew if they spent the night in the condo with only the cats and television for entertainment, he'd eventually begin asking questions, and maybe even start a fight. The better thing to do would be keep busy while the dust settled on her request.

"It's such a nice night, we should go out to dinner."

She glanced at him with a smile. "Okay."

Her smile warmed him, sent him back to the weeks before they'd slept together, back to the friendship he loved. Guilt at his nagging suspicions about her shamed him. She'd never asked for a favor or special treatment. He should trust her.

Except his business instincts were telling him there was something personal behind her request.

Battling it out in his brain was exhausting. He needed a night of peace.

He set his briefcase down so he could help her into her coat. "I know just the place for us to eat. I'll have Timothy call and get us a reservation and by the time we arrive, our table will be ready."

She shook her head. "So pampered."

"I like to think of it as my reward for being a hard worker."

She said, "Eh," and walked with him to the elevator. They rode to the first floor, got out in the lobby and headed to his limo parked on the street. Neither one said a word, but it didn't feel odd or awkward. That lifted his mood and silenced his suspicions.

Sam, a seasoned driver with a wicked sense of

humor, opened the car door for them. "Evening, sir." He touched the rim of his cap. "Ma'am."

They slid inside. "I feel so old when someone calls me ma'am."

"You are old. You're over thirty."

She laughed. "I'm just thirty."

He gave her the side-eye as he corrected her. "Thirty-one."

"That's still the beginning of the thirties. It's not like I'm thirty-two like you are."

He rolled his eyes at her teasing and relaxed even more. Eleanora would not cheat him, would not lie to him, would not take advantage of him—

Unless her wanting to move around had something to do with their child?

He groaned internally and told himself to stop obsessing. They ate a leisurely dinner at a restaurant near Times Square, but because they'd gone to eat directly from the office, it was early when they were done. Not wanting to give his brain any more time to fixate on why she'd asked for a promotion, he suggested they walk to Times Square.

Meandering through the thin crowd, she took a long, slow breath. "I love this place."

"You just like the lights."

She looked around. "And the people."

"Not so many people out tonight."

"Yeah."

The street wasn't deserted but it wasn't crowded as it would be in a few weeks when hordes of Christmas shoppers would descend.

Snowflakes began to dance around them. "It's snowing."

She glanced at him. "Meaning, you want to go back to the limo?"

"No. If you're enjoying this—"

"I am. I love winter in Manhattan. Though, I have to admit I'm looking forward to seeing what winter in Rome is like."

His brain tweaked. A woman who loved Rome shouldn't be asking to be transferred. Of course, her transfer wouldn't take place until at least eighteen months from now.

Then she'd be back in the corporate office for a few months, as part of the planning and design team—

Maybe she was trying to find a way to bring them together, a way to subtly move herself into the corporate office, at least part-time? That was better than thinking she was using him somehow or taking advantage of his promise that her pregnancy wouldn't hold her back in her career.

"You don't remember winter in Rome from last year?"

She laughed. "You don't remember how busy we were?" She sucked in a breath, seeming to enjoy the brisk air. "Besides, I wasn't there permanently. I did a lot of flying back and forth through the construction phase."

Which would be ridiculously difficult for a woman with a child! Damn it! Why was his brain so fixated on this?

"And you want to go back to that in Paris?"

She shrugged. "Sort of. It seems like so much fun to be the one who breathes life into your ideas and to live in the most wonderful cities in the world."

"But you're not sure?"

"It's something we need to think about, consider all angles, make the best decision for the company."

He almost said, "Thank you," but he always knew she had the best interest of the company in mind. He shouldn't have doubted her. He shouldn't have wondered about *her* taking the position as a new mother.

He should have trusted her.

It wasn't the first time he'd thought that. So, he anchored that thought in the front of his brain. No matter what, he should trust her. He'd always trusted her. Always liked her. Being suspicious of her made him feel like a louse when she was such a good person.

Silence stretched between them. The strangest urge to catch her hand filled him. Not wanting it, he shoved his hand in his overcoat pocket. "Anyway, I'm glad you think ahead. I'm glad you think about more than your job. It's why we picked you to be manager of our first European hotel. We wanted someone special."

And she was special.

The thought sneaked up on him before he could stop it, filling him with warmth. The feelings that accompanied it weren't friendly, happy feelings and they especially were not boss-like. They were tingly, intimate—

Maybe a moonlight walk on one of the world's prettiest streets wasn't so wise after all?

"You know what? It's cold enough now that I think we should get back to the limo."

She turned without argument. "Okay." She peeked at him. "Race you?"

"What?"

She was three feet ahead of him by the time he realized she was serious. They ran up the street to the limo and were laughing when they reached it. Even in heels she'd almost beaten him.

Having surprised Sam, he wasn't at the door to open it, and they slid to the back fender, leaning against it to catch their breath.

Sam came outside shaking his head. "You two are nuts."

They burst out laughing. Eleanora said, "We know."

Sam opened the door. "Get in. It's colder than it was supposed to be."

"We saw snowflakes," Eleanora said excitedly.

"Peachy."

He closed the door. Eleanora and Marco exchanged a look, then burst out laughing again. In another almost automatic move, he nearly put his arm around her and hugged her to him.

But that wasn't boss-like either. Or friendly. He wasn't entirely sure what it was, but the ease and simplicity of the instinct that continually sneaked up on him was going to catch him off guard one day and he was going to do something like kiss her again.

Sam drove them to Marco's building. They told him goodnight before they entered and rode the elevator to his penthouse. As soon as he switched on the lights, Sunrise and Sunset woke, yawning and stretching on his sofa.

Eleanora gasped. "We forgot to feed them!"

"I texted Wisdom. Because I never know when I'll be getting home, she's always on call."

She walked over to the cats, scratched both of their heads, then shrugged out of her coat. "Did you guys have fun today?"

They looked at her as if fun was a foreign concept. But as soon as she sat on the sofa, both crawled onto her lap. "I think you missed me."

Sunrise ran his face along her chin. Sunset gazed up at her and purred.

She scratched their heads again. "Sweet boys."

"I never took you for a cat person."

She glanced at him. "I love cats. Cats are happy you're home, but they'll gaze at you adoringly rather than expend the energy to knock you over at the door the way dogs will."

He laughed. "I totally agree." He walked to the open bar. "Mind if I have a drink?"

"No. Go ahead." She rose from the sofa, depositing both cats on the cushions beside her. "In fact, I'm going to my room. I want a shower and maybe ten minutes to read before I fall asleep. At the rate I'm going, it will take me until spring before I finish this novel."

He said, "Okay." But another of those weird urges hit him, as she passed him on the way to her room. He could catch her hand and kiss her goodnight. Easily. Automatically.

He cursed in his head. He did not want to confuse their situation after he'd so clearly explained things or have her rightfully yell at him, yet these urges formed as naturally as a breath.

He shook his head to clear it. As Eleanora's bedroom door closed, he pulled his phone from his pocket and fell to the sofa beside Sunrise and Sunset.

Their heads tilted in unison, and they stared at him.

"I know. You'd rather have the pretty girl sitting beside you."

Sunrise sniffed the air. Sunset plopped down again.

He glanced at the texts on his phone. Two from Chiara. He'd texted to ask her where she was, and her vague reply gave him a funny feeling in the pit of his stomach. She wasn't so dim-witted that she wouldn't understand his question. Yet, her response totally avoided it.

He tried to call her but got no answer. Rising from the sofa, he walked to the bar and retrieved the bourbon he'd poured. He sent Chiara two more texts: one asking where she was—again— and the other referencing their trip to Vermont to be with their dad for the Christmas holiday.

She didn't reply. Not knowing what part of the world she was in, he had to acknowledge that she might be sleeping. Still, he waited a half hour for a reply, focusing on the phone, hoping she wasn't avoiding him because she planned to bail on the Christmas reunion that their dad was looking forward to.

That was better than thinking about Eleanora showering, then sliding between the soft sheets just down the hall.

He could easily picture her naked with her

head on the pillow, her auburn hair a pretty contrast to the white case, because that's what she'd looked like when he'd left her the morning after their tryst.

He pushed himself up off the sofa and tossed his bourbon into the sink before he headed to his room. With her at his fingertips, remembering how she looked in bed was not a wise move, especially since they had a long weekend with no work to keep them busy.

CHAPTER EIGHT

THE FOLLOWING MONDAY MORNING, Eleanora walked into the main room of the penthouse with her suitcase. Their race to the limo after their walk to Times Square had made her giddy and happy and that was wrong. Nothing was going to happen between them and she needed to let all that sink in.

Plus, Marco avoided her so much over the weekend that they weren't discussing their issues. She had a new hotel that was running okay without her, but she wanted to see that for herself. On top of that, she had a new perspective on her life to think through. She'd made a suggestion about creating a position in the company for her and she was positive that was what had made Marco quiet.

Lots had happened and they needed time apart to let some of it to settle. They needed to decide what was best for each of them individually before they started discussions on how to handle the parts of their lives that would have to mesh.

"I'm going back to Rome for a week. We're not making much progress here. A little time apart to sort all this out will probably do us some good."

He glanced at her over the rim of his coffee cup, and she braced herself for an argument. But he said, "Okay. See you Friday?"

She had to school her face to keep her surprise from showing. He was such a bossy guy she couldn't believe he was letting her leave when he'd said she would be staying until they figured out their situation—

Except, she was the manager of his newest hotel. The businessman in him was probably glad she was taking real in-person time to do her job.

"How about next Monday? I'll fly out of Rome Monday morning and get here Monday morning your time."

"Sounds good."

She smiled as she wheeled her suitcase to the elevator, but an unexpected loneliness filled her as she got off in the lobby. On the ride to the airport, she told herself she was crazy. She didn't belong here. She wasn't sure where she belonged but setting up all the Grand York's European hotels still felt like something she should be doing.

It took her two days in Italy to get accustomed to the time change. Coupling pregnancy exhaustion with jet lag, she was barely coherent. But when she went to her Grand York Hotel on Thursday morning, she saw the whispering and strange glances from her staff. Tiredness had kept her from seeing it on Tuesday or Wednesday, but that morning she saw it all clearly.

She hadn't forgotten Sheila had overheard her and Marco talking about a pregnancy. She knew the whole staff had seen them dancing and having fun at the grand opening. She couldn't tell if they'd put two and two together yet. But it didn't matter. It wasn't time to tell her staff *she* was the person who was pregnant. And it might never be time to tell them Marco was her baby's father. That could end up being none of their business. Especially if she moved on to the Paris hotel.

More than that, though, she didn't know how involved Marco wanted to be with their baby. She didn't know if he would want staff to know he'd fathered a child with an employee. She wasn't the kind of person to be secretive, but she did recognize this pregnancy came with some issues for him and suddenly saw that might be why he hadn't yet figured out what he wanted to do or how he wanted to handle everything.

A little more understanding of Marco's hesitation, she showed up at the corporate office for Grand York the following Monday ready to talk.

But she didn't even see Marco until it was time to go home. It could have struck her as odd, except everything about their situation was odd.

Unfortunately, when he came looking for her after six that night, when it was time to go home, her heart skipped a beat.

She didn't want to have missed him, but she had. She missed how sexy he looked with the sleeves of his white shirt rolled up to his elbows. She missed his smile. His voice. How he loved his job, his family's company.

Damn it. She pretty much loved everything about him.

His suit coat in one hand, he unrolled the sleeves of his shirt with the other. "Hey! Timothy told me you were back!"

Her unruly heart stuttered. She knew how wrong it was to have missed him, but she had.

"Ready to go home?"

She nodded and rose as he retrieved her coat and helped her into it. After he shrugged into his suit coat, he grabbed the handle of her rolling suitcase and walked with her to the elevator.

"How was Rome?"

"Great." She considered telling him about the weird looks and whispers but decided all that was irrelevant. Gossip was gossip. But it did point out that they needed to make some decisions. "I'm not sure if I should be proud or upset that everything runs so smoothly without me."

He shrugged as they stepped into the elevator. "A place that runs well without the leader usually means the leader has taught her staff well."

"I hope."

After they'd settle into the back seat of the limo, he asked a few more questions about the Rome hotel. He got specific, but luckily she'd studied the financials so much the week before she'd all but memorized them.

The questions continued as they rode up the elevator to the penthouse. The car stopped. The doors opened.

He stepped out, rolling her case. She stayed right behind him so that she could grab her luggage when he released it and head back to the bedroom to change out of clothes she felt like she'd been wearing forever.

"One more thing." He let go of the case. But instead of stepping to the right or left, he turned to her and suddenly they were face-to-face, six inches apart.

Their gazes caught. All the feelings she'd had when he walked into her office tumbled through her. How much she'd missed him. How handsome he was. How great he looked and smelled—and felt. She knew all that because they'd been intimate. And now they were pretending it hadn't happened.

"Oops! Sorry!" He jumped back as if touching her would burn him. "Let me get your bag back to your room, then we'll order dinner."

His phone buzzed. He grabbed it from his jacket pocket. He said, "Give me a second," before he clicked to answer. "Marco Pearson."

He paused, listening, then winced. "I'm so sorry. I totally forgot about you. But I'm available to talk now." He walked around the kitchen island, opened a drawer and pulled out three take-out menus. "Hold on a sec."

Putting his call on hold, he handed the menus to Eleanora. "Order whatever you want and add something with chicken for me. Then ring Arnie to let him know it's coming."

She nodded but she wasn't even sure he'd seen. He reconnected his call, grabbed the handle of her bag and started down the hall again.

Sunrise and Sunset watched her as she glanced at the menus, then phoned in an order. As if waiting for her to finish, they wrapped around her ankles and meowed their happiness to see her.

She gave each a handful of treats and laughed as they gobbled them down. "You just like me because I feed you—"

Which was exactly what Marco had said her

first night in the penthouse when they reacted so crazy happy to see Wisdom.

She frowned. Marco might not have come to see her until it was time to leave the office for the day, but he'd been chatty, asking questions about the hotel. He hadn't gotten quiet until they'd come here, and he'd almost bumped into her when he turned around to ask a question.

Maybe he'd missed her too?

She told herself not to think like that. Those thoughts were counterproductive to them having a good discussion about their child. And they needed to talk about her pregnancy, the baby, visitation, custody, *everything*.

Walking back to her room, she put thoughts of Marco out of her head. The door to his office was closed, meaning his call was important. She changed her clothes and went out to the main room to play with the cats again.

After a week of hearing the constant chatter from her Rome employees, the penthouse was too quiet. Worse, she didn't want to think about Marco, not her attraction or his odd reaction to almost bumping into her. So, she took the happy-to-see-her cats for a walk. In the lobby, she told Arnie to hang on to her food when it arrived and she headed outside, two happy cats on their leashes.

New York City typically burst with life and energy. But in Marco's exclusive residential corner, all that seemed far away, as trees lost leaves and the air became a little colder every day. Thanksgiving was now a little less than two weeks away. She'd soon be telling her parents she was pregnant.

Relief hit her. That end of the secrecy would be over. Then all she'd have to worry about was the people she and Marco worked with. Because those choices affected him more than her, she'd decided they'd share whatever he wanted to be shared and nothing more.

When she returned from her walk with the cats, Marco was still behind the closed door of his office. Not wanting to disturb him, she texted that their food had arrived, but he never came out. She ate and put his food in the refrigerator, then went to her room.

Rolling out of bed the next morning in the silent penthouse, she almost let discomfort overwhelm her. Instead, she counted her blessings that her pregnancy hadn't made her sick, dressed for a day at work and went to the kitchen, where Marco sat at the center island reading his phone.

Without looking up, Marco said, "I bought bagels." He pointed at a bag sitting on the kitchen island.

It was the most words he'd spoken to her that

weren't about work. Actually, those were the *only* words he'd spoken that weren't about work.

She told herself not to question his withdrawal because she realized the stress of their pregnancy impacted him differently from how it impacted her, but something about it felt weird. Normally when he was worried about anything, business or personal, he'd seek her advice. Worse, she was only here, in his city and his penthouse, so they could discuss how to handle her pregnancy. His withdrawal didn't make any sense.

She decided to tease him and see if that didn't get him back to normal. "You mean you *ordered* bagels."

"Nope. Couldn't sleep. Got out of bed and found an all-night bagel shop."

Recognizing this was her opening, she took a bagel from the container, popped it in the toaster and leaned against the countertop as she waited for it to brown. "Why couldn't you sleep?"

He peered up at her. His gaze went from her head to her feet so quickly she wouldn't have noticed it if she had been doing anything other than wait for her bagel to toast.

"I was thinking about things."

She didn't think the look was sexual. He was a man of his word. Though he'd slipped when he'd kissed her, he'd promised that wouldn't happen again. So there'd be nothing sexual between them. Not even looks.

"Thinking about things like work?"

"Like baby names and good schools."

She perked up, thrilled he was ready to start discussing their child. "What did you come up with?"

"So far not much."

"Is that what you're searching on your phone?"

"No, I'm texting Chiara."

Even better. Eleanora liked his sister. If he was moody or unhappy, his sister could always cheer him up. "How is she?"

"She's great." He rose from his seat. Wearing gray trousers and a white shirt, he'd obviously dressed for work.

Her mouth watered. It was ridiculous to be attracted to a guy who didn't want her, and maybe even a little odd to be so turned on by a guy in a suit, but she was. She agreed with everything he'd said about not wanting to be in a relationship, but this morning, he just looked yummy. She knew increased sex drive was a side effect of being pregnant—but she'd never needed a reason to find Marco attractive.

She pulled in a breath. Told herself to stop thinking of him that way. Then she wondered why. If she really had decided to stop looking for a once-in-a-lifetime love, then what did it matter if she fantasized a little?

"Did you tell her about the baby?"

"No." He grabbed his phone and walked back to his room.

Well, that was abrupt.

The toaster signaled that her bagel was done. She got cream cheese and slathered it all over the warm bread. She took a bite, let it settle on her taste buds deliciously and groaned with happiness.

When he came out, she was finished eating and licking cream cheese from her fingers. He caught her and she winced. "It's just so darned good. Everything tastes better since I got pregnant."

He smiled woodenly.

"Oh, come on. I've got to be able to talk about the weirdness of pregnancy with you. You're the only one who knows. Plus, weeks have gone by since I told you we were going to have a baby and we've decided nothing. I think it's time we started talking about things."

"That's why I was thinking about baby names this morning." He pulled his suit coat off the back of his chair by the island and slid into it. "We'll hit it hard when we get home from work tonight."

Again, his voice was flat, almost as if he were

discussing new dish towels for the restaurant kitchen. She should have been confused, but he looked so damned good in that suit that her hormones sat up and wanted to say, "Hey, sailor." And the only way to battle that back was to keep her focus on their conversation.

"Honestly, I think baby names is a great place to start. It will ground us to the reality of having a child, so things won't be so abstract."

"Okay. We'll do that tonight."

His continued coolness made her frown. But she reminded herself that pregnancy hormones could be to blame for her being so nit-picky about his moods too. "Okay."

"I'm taking the limo. I'll send Sam back for you."

She shrugged. "Okay."

He left on the elevator, and she watched until the door closed behind him. Thinking about how good he'd looked that morning, she sighed dreamily, then cursed herself. For heaven's sake. They'd made the decision not to form a romance. She had to stop noticing everything about him and halfway swooning over him.

She walked back to her room, reapplied her lipstick and waited for Sam to call to let her know he had returned from taking Marco.

This time when she frowned it wasn't from emotion. Technically, she was ready for work.

All he had to do was look at her to see that. But he hadn't even suggested she get her coat and ride with him.

As if he didn't want her in his car?

That was stupid.

He rode home with her that night, negating her odd feeling that he was avoiding her. When they arrived at the penthouse, he ordered Chinese food for dinner, and she went back to her bedroom to change into something more comfortable.

She slid into black yoga pants and reached for a big T-shirt but in the last second changed her mind and grabbed a tank top. She pulled it over her head, then smoothed it over her still-slim torso. Not that she wanted to look sexy for him—well, maybe a little. It didn't seem fair that while she was fighting hormones, he was going on business as usual.

His eyebrows rose when she sidled up to the center island in the kitchen, but he said nothing. Arnie the doorman called to say their food had arrived and he would bring it up.

As Marco set down his phone, Eleanora smiled at him. Just the thought of getting food had subdued her hormones and if that wasn't a reason to smile, she didn't know what was.

He sucked in a breath and turned on his heel

to face the elevator when the bell rang announcing its arrival.

Arnie stepped out. Looking past Marco, he said, "Evening, Eleanora."

"Evening, Arnie."

Marco took the containers. "Thanks."

Arnie said, "Any time," got back in the elevator and left.

She sniffed the air. "Oh, that smells great!"

Marco glanced at her. The joy on her pretty face was enough to tempt a man, but as she sniffed, her chest puffed out, the little tank top expanded, showing off her breasts—which he knew were as soft as heaven.

He turned to the cupboards. "Let's get plates."

"Too late. I opened the orange chicken and took a piece."

He peered at her over his shoulder. "You're getting a plate anyway."

She licked her fingers clean of the orange sauce. He turned back to the cupboard and squeezed his eyes shut. She was killing him.

They ate in silence, which he had decided was the best way to deal with his voice that grew husky or wanted to squeak every time he looked at her.

Or she laughed.

Or she licked her fingers.

Or she just sat there breathing.

He'd thought the time away from each other while she was in Rome would ease his attraction. Instead, memories of the softness of her skin on the inside of her thighs, the scent of her shampoo, the silkiness of her hair sliding through his fingers wafted into his brain. Rather than his attraction diminishing, he'd begun remembering even more detail than he had the day after their night together.

He strode around her to get out of the kitchen. "There's a game on tonight. I think I'll watch."

She finished stacking her dishes in the dishwasher and stood in between the kitchen and living areas, as if confused.

He said nothing. He didn't want to encourage her to sit beside him. Being apart hadn't helped his feelings and he really needed some space.

"Okay. I'll go read."

He didn't look at her. "Good night."

She left for her bedroom, but her scent stayed. He cursed it. Then he remembered he'd told her they'd discuss baby names. That was his salvation. No matter how big the potential that they would hit some roadblocks when they tried to figure out how people who lived on two continents raised a child, at least that would get his mind off the fact that he'd like nothing better than to fall into bed with her.

The next morning Marco found her at the kitchen island eating a bagel. Busying himself getting a cup of coffee, he said, "I was thinking we should name our baby Joshua if he's a boy."

She perked up. Wearing a sweater over black wool pants, she should simply look professional. But he saw only a bundle of softness as her scent drifted to him.

"Aw. Your dad's name, which is very sweet, but if we name our baby after your dad my dad might feel slighted."

He winced. "Never thought of that."

"Did you come up with a girl's name?"

As he'd hoped, delving into a real discussion corralled his attraction. Leaning against the counter, with a cup of coffee warming his fingers, he said, "How about Margarita?"

"You want to name your child after a drink with tequila?"

"It's also a very pretty name."

"Margarite is. But Margarita is a drink that makes people act crazy. Imagine the teasing she'll get in high school." She rose from her seat. "I'm going to get my stuff. We can ride to work together this morning."

He smiled and nodded, but when she was out of sight he groaned. Not only had she stopped the names discussion, but he was doing a terrible job of maintaining distance between them.

Luckily, talking about baby names had kept his mind off a million things he'd like to do with her.

Tonight, if they stalled on baby names, he'd bring up custody and visitation. It might start an argument but maybe that would be a good thing? Maybe he wouldn't be so attracted to her if he remembered there were some serious decisions that could potentially make them adversaries.

Feeling more in control, he rode with her to the office. They parted ways in the reception area. He spent the next hour preparing for a meeting with his vice presidents, then spent the meeting focused on reports and discussions.

When the meeting could have ended, he sat back in his chair. "I have some new business. Eleanora approached me with an idea and I'm not sure how I feel about it."

His vice presidents looked at him expectantly.

"After her experiences with the Rome hotel, she suggested that we might want to consider having her take over the Paris hotel at the same point where she joined the Rome team."

Sally Jenkins frowned. "She's not happy in Rome?"

"No. She loves it. But I think she likes the process of planning and building and setting everything up for a grand opening."

This time *everybody* frowned.

Bob Marin shifted on his chair. "It sounds like she's suggesting we create a new position."

"You have to admit it has merit."

Sally inclined her head, saying, "Maybe."

His oldest vice president, Orville Santangelo, said, "She would ultimately become an expert at finishing the developmental phase and setting up the hotel for a grand opening."

"I think that's her motivation." Marco began to gather his things. "Okay. Meeting's adjourned. We'll finish this discussion later. I told you today because I want you all to think about it. We'll all spend a week considering the ins and outs and what works and what doesn't and then we'll talk again next week."

Sally said, "I'm happy to consider it but, honestly, Marco, Eleanora isn't the person for the job."

"She might not know construction," Marco quickly said, defending her. "But she's not looking at the building from a construction standpoint when she suggests changing something in the plans. She'll be looking at it from a hotel manager's vantage point to make things run more smoothly or efficiently. The construction team will take it from there."

Sally sighed and leaned back on her chair.

"Marco, that's not the problem. You know she's pregnant, right?"

Marco froze but recovered quickly. He had to. He was Eleanora's only advocate. "Yes. We're friends. She tells me things."

Sally said, "The point where she'd join the Paris team would dovetail with her having a nine-month-old child."

"Are you suggesting we discriminate against her because she'll soon be a mother?"

"No. I'm saying we don't know how her pregnancy will turn out."

"With a baby?"

"Don't be obtuse, Marco. Not all pregnancies go smoothly. Not all children are born healthy."

He fell to his seat. His entire team stared at him. He and Eleanora were friends. Sally had risked angering him and they all knew it. What they didn't know was that he was her baby's father and suggesting something might be wrong with *his* child froze his chest, sent fear tumbling through him.

He rose clumsily, so eager to leave that he could barely gather his things. "Okay. Let's consider her idea generically. If it works, then she *will* be considered as the first person to hold the position."

"Marco," Sally said patiently. "I know you want to avoid a lawsuit, but you have to be realistic. There are a million reasons we can say she didn't fit the position. We're not stuck with her because she came up with the idea."

"No. I suppose we're not. But I like to think our company is fair. So she *will* be considered to be the first one to hold the position."

The room fell silent as he headed for the door. He caught the knob but shook his head and faced his executive board again.

He almost told them he was the baby's father but knew that would come with tons of trouble. Not the least of which might be an accusation of partiality to Eleanora. Not only that, but if he told them, the news would get back to his dad and he wanted to tell his dad himself.

He couldn't believe he was just recognizing these things now and suddenly realized how much he was on the outside looking in with this pregnancy. Not only was he not involved enough to consider all angles, to consider that things might go wrong, but he was letting Eleanora down.

For all the searching he'd done on raising a child, becoming a parent, he'd only hit the tip of the iceberg when it came to pregnancy.

CHAPTER NINE

WHEN MARCO ARRIVED home that night, he raced out of the elevator. Frowning, Eleanora set her book on her lap. "What's up?"

"I went looking for you to ride home and you were already gone."

Which shouldn't be an issue. They didn't always ride together. In fact, he was the one who started that trend. "I got a wave of exhaustion that almost put me to sleep so I came home, had a nap and finished up my work from here."

He nodded as he shrugged out of his overcoat and removed his scarf. November had gotten cold. But frankly, he looked so good dressed up like the successful businessman that he was that she loved him in a scarf and overcoat.

"I think the nap was a good idea." He walked over to the sofa and sat on the arm. "But I want to make sure you're not sick."

"No. I was just tired."

"I mean, if you were sick, you'd tell me. Right?"

"Who did I call when I went to the emergency room in Rome?"

"Me."

"You'll always be my first call."

He seemed to be placated and rose from the sofa's arm, heading for the kitchen area. "Have anything special you'd like for dinner?"

"I wouldn't mind another toasted cheese sandwich."

He laughed, but it sounded forced, as if his heart wasn't in it. Still, he let her have the kitchen to make the toasted cheese sandwiches. But the questions about how she was feeling started again as they ate. Worse, they continued throughout the week. First, he'd brought up preeclampsia and asked if there was a history of diabetes in her family. Then, he'd talked about high blood pressure, asking if she had any dizziness. Then, he sent her emails on warning signs for placenta previa. She was positive his phone was wearing out from searching for every imaginable thing that could go wrong.

By Friday she was exhausted from assuring him everything was fine. When he walked into Eleanora's little office an hour before normal quitting time, she almost groaned. Especially when he set his overcoat and briefcase on the chair in front of her desk and walked to the coat tree holding her jacket.

"Let's go."

"Go? Leave work? Right now?"

"Tonight, we are going to talk."

She snorted. "All we've been doing all week is talk, but not about the right stuff."

"I know we started talking baby names on Monday, but something happened that afternoon that sort of threw me."

"You should stop Googling things. There's a difference between being prepared and needlessly scaring yourself." She thought for a second. "Unless somebody else scared you."

He didn't say anything, simply stood there holding her jacket, and she rolled the possibilities around in her head.

"Who said something?" She paused. "Who in the corporate office even *knows*?"

"Maybe more people than you think. Someone brought it up at our executive meeting on Monday."

She gasped. She'd think someone from her staff squealed, except none of them were involved with executive staff. Unless Sheila talked to the assistant of someone on the executive board?

Still, how did it come up at a meeting of vice presidents? "How the hell did *I* come up at an executive meeting?"

"I mentioned your idea about a hotel manager who opens all our European hotels."

That was sort of flattering, sort of concerning, given that he'd walked away from that meeting upset. "I see."

"No. You don't. The conversation was dry as toast until they suggested that we needed to be sure everything was fine with your pregnancy before we considered shifting you around."

"Oh, Marco..." He wouldn't have been prepared for the insinuation that something might be wrong with their baby. That's why it threw him. That's why he'd researched every bad pregnancy thing possible. "Is that what happened? They planted a bad seed about my pregnancy?"

"They reminded me that not all pregnancies go smoothly."

"That's true but we're both very healthy and our baby's heart was strong. I've got that list of obstetricians from the ER doctor in Italy. As soon as I go back, I'll give one a call."

"I think we should have a doctor here too."

"Really?"

"Why not?"

"Because I'm going back to Rome soon. I can't stay here."

"Why? You haven't yet told your parents. Thursday is Thanksgiving. Why not do it then? In fact, I can come with you to Thanksgiving dinner. We can tell them together."

She let that idea sink in. "I had planned on telling them at Thanksgiving dinner."

"We'll use it as our perfect opportunity to get the ball rolling on telling our families."

"Okay." She peeked at him. "So we're good?"

He opened her jacket for her to slide into it. "Our Thanksgiving plans are good. Your place as the manager who opens all European hotels isn't."

"They didn't like the idea?"

"They loved the idea. They're just not sure about you. I didn't appreciate the way they dissected your life to make sure you suit our purposes."

She pondered that, as she picked up her purse and briefcase. "Isn't that their job?"

"Yes. But—"

It was no wonder he'd been so odd all week. He'd lost his objectivity. "No *buts*. The primary reason to have advisers is so they can tear ideas apart to make sure they're worthy. Relax. Let them work through this so they can provide you with the facts. Then you make the choice."

She slid her arm beneath his and directed him to walk up the hall to the elevator. Tonight might not be the night to discuss custody or visitation. He needed some time to chill.

"How about if I buy you dinner?"

"That's okay. I can—"

"Shush. This is one of our friend things, remember? We're equals. Sometimes you pay. Sometimes I pay." She laughed. "Besides, this way I get to choose the place."

He pressed the button for the elevator, then turned so she could see him roll his eyes. "You can always choose the place. You know I love everything."

The door opened and they stepped inside the elevator. "I do know that."

"What are you hungry for?"

"Toasted cheese sandwiches."

He shook his head. "No. Since your choice is repetitive and bad, I'm vetoing that in favor of a steak."

"Steak sounds good."

He took her to an Italian restaurant famous for its *bistecca alla fiorentina* and they indulged. Walking up the street to his limo after, they passed a bakery and he darted inside to purchase half a dozen bagels, four Danish pastries and six doughnuts.

As they stepped out into the cold night, she laughed. "Buy yourself a midnight snack?"

"It's potential breakfasts for you."

Her stomach sat up and took notice. "All those doughnuts are mine?"

"Anything you want is yours." Rather than turn left to get to his car, he hesitated. "We're close to Rockefeller Center. How about we go over and watch the skaters?"

This suggestion made her frown. It was as if he didn't want to go home. "Is Wisdom going to care for Sunrise and Sunset?"

"I texted her."

He definitely wasn't ready to go home. She'd thought talking out the things from the executive board meeting had helped him settle, and she believed the delicious steak had taken the last steps to putting him in a good mood.

But he was still antsy.

Something other than his board's reaction to her suggestion about managing all the European hotels was bothering him.

"Then let's go watch people skate."

They walked the few blocks in the cold night. Lights illuminated Rockefeller Center and the space around it. She looked up at the tall buildings that surrounded the skating rink. Any time she came here to skate or just to watch, she always felt like she was cocooned in a private world, a fairyland with the flags and statues and happy skaters.

"Too bad we can't see the stars."

He glanced at her. "What?"

His face was shadowed, but she could still see the sculptured features, his serious brown eyes. Other people might not find his seriousness sexy, but she did. The way he worried about their baby tugged at her heartstrings, but the way he looked after her filled her with longing. She wanted to be able to cuddle against him, to talk about their baby as their baby, not custody or visitation rights. She wanted to whisper possibilities in the dark as they lay together in his bed.

The longing became an earthy need. This tall, gorgeous, strong man was the father of her child and she wanted to enjoy that to the fullest. To be lovers planning the birth of their baby—

But he didn't.

She took a breath and pointed up. "The city lights block out the stars." They were quiet a second, then she said, "I've done some traveling in Italy, taken some weekends and enjoyed the countryside. I liked seeing the stars. Natural. Shiny. As if they're smiling down on us."

He snorted. "We're two city kids who can be wowed by the world."

She nudged him with her shoulder. "Or maybe we're two lucky city kids who get wonderful opportunities."

He leaned against the wrought iron rail, his hands folded in front of him. "Yeah. We are."

She leaned down, sliding her arm beneath his so she could nestle against him, the way they always did when they talked seriously.

Warmth filled her, along with the crazy need to be with him, to enjoy every naked inch of him. She jerked away, pretending the snuggle was a quick friendly hug before he noticed her breath had stalled.

Bringing the conversation back, she said, "We are both lucky, and now we're going to have a baby."

He sucked in a breath. "Yeah."

She shook her head. His serious demeanor was really turning her on. Because she loved that about him? Loved that he was strong and smart? Or because the guy being serious was the best-looking, best-built guy she'd ever met?

It could go either way.

Fighting the hormones and fantasies, she said, "Okay. I've worked all the angles to help you get back to being chipper and happy. But I still hear something in your voice. What's the matter?"

"Truth?"

"Yes!"

"You are the one carrying the baby. You know how you feel. If you're sick, you can take care of yourself. If you're tired, you take a nap."

Confusion made her face scrunch. "And that's bad?"

"No. I just have this sense that I'm on the out-side looking in. I don't know when you're hungry. I don't know when you're tired. I don't know when you're sick."

That explained all the questions from the week before and the doughnuts, Danish pastries and bagels. But that was the price they paid for keeping their distance—which was his choice.

She sighed. "I don't know how to fix that."

"I don't either."

"I can tell you this. Stop Googling things. Unless I mention that I have a symptom, don't look for trouble."

He laughed.

They watched the skaters for another fifteen minutes, then they walked to his limo and went home.

Giving him time to digest everything she'd said, she immediately went to her bedroom and stripped for a shower, but while she was running a soapy cloth over herself, she saw that her abdomen had swollen. She smiled, then a thought hit her. She turned off the spray, dried and jumped into loose pajamas.

Racing into the front room, she didn't see Marco. Both cats were on the sofa, so she knew he hadn't decided on an evening stroll. She headed back to the primary bedroom and knocked lightly on the door.

"Marco?"

"Yeah?"

"Are you decent?"

"Yes."

She opened the door and stepped inside. He stood at the foot of the bed. His jacket, tie, shoes and socks were gone, as if he was preparing to take a shower. That crazy need rippled through her again. Warm and sensual, it snaked through her bloodstream. She'd seen him like this before, but all those innocent images paled, and she remembered the night of the grand opening. Watching him unbutton his shirt, swoosh away his tie, kick his shoes across the room.

She swallowed hard. Forcing herself to remember her mission, she walked over to him, caught his hand and put it on her stomach. "Feel that?"

He looked at her as if she were crazy.

"It's a baby bump."

A surprised laugh escaped him. "Oh."

She let go of his hand. "It's better as a visual." Lifting her pajama top a bit, she took his hand again and laid it on the actual bump. He could now see the small swell as he felt it.

He caught her gaze. "That's amazing."

"Nah. It's only a few centimeters." She smiled but didn't move or lift his hand, letting him soak in the experience, driving herself just a little bit crazy in order to ease his mind.

His voice a hushed whisper, Marco said, "That's our baby."

"That's our baby."

His head tilted. "You seem really happy."

"I am." She held his gaze to make sure he heard and believed what she was about to say. In the stillness of his bedroom, honesty seemed to come easier. Truth insisted on being told. Apprehension bubbled through her, but she pushed it down. This was their moment of truth. She only hoped she had the courage to carry it through to the right conclusion.

"Like we said at Rockefeller Center, we are lucky. Maybe luckier than we even think."

He frowned, not quite sure what she was getting at.

"After you explained why you didn't want a committed relationship, I did some soul searching about my own life. I realized I'm happy with what I have too. All my experiences with men have sort of shown me that maybe I don't want that happily-ever-after love. And when I think that thought through to its logical conclusion, I realize this baby is the next step in my life." She laughed. "I'm going to be a mom."

He studied her glowing face. "You're saying that if you take the happily-ever-after out of the equation, your life is right on target?"

"Yes!" Another joyful laugh escaped her. "I'm exactly where I'm supposed to be and I'm almost giddy about it. I don't know if it's pregnancy hormones or if it's the decision to love my life as it is, but something finally made me see that I have everything I want. Not just pride in my professional life. But I look around at my condo in Rome, my friends, my family...and now a baby?" She shrugged. "I have it all."

He chuckled. "Then it looks like we both have it all."

"We do!"

The room grew silent. She stood in front of him the very proud mother of his child. His hand still rested on the small swell of her stomach. And he didn't feel like he was on the outside anymore. The emotional distance between them melted into nothing.

Knowing they were treading into dangerous territory, he started to turn away again, but she stopped him by putting her hand on his elbow. "I'm not done with everything I need to say." She took a quick breath. "I'm glad you're my baby's father. Yeah, we have some stuff to work out...but think of the losers I've dated."

He burst out laughing.

"I'm serious. You're my best friend, Marco. There's no one else I'd rather raise a child with." She pointed her index finger at him. "You're not going to railroad me over visitation or custody. It's going to be a challenge to figure that out. But we'll figure it out. When it comes to who I want teaching my little boy or girl about life, about holidays, about fishing and cabins and making good decisions, I couldn't have chosen anybody better than you."

His heart turned over in his chest. When she put it that way, he realized he couldn't think of anybody he'd rather have as the mother of his child.

"I couldn't have chosen anybody better than you either."

"We're going to be great parents."

He snorted. "I haven't spent a holiday with my dad in three years. My sister and I communicate through texts and occasional calls. I'm just peachy."

"Your family went through something. And everybody handles grief differently. You never stopped loving your dad, never lost touch with your sister. You held on when another person might have walked away."

"My dad's so eager for our Christmas reunion and I'm afraid Chiara's going to bail. I can't even blame her. There are days I wish I had any other plans than to go back to the place that reminds me the most of my mom."

"But you're going."

He inclined his head. "I'm going."

"And that's part of what makes you such a great guy. You understand responsibility. You understand more about family than you think you do."

That explained his protective feelings for her and his sudden longing to be a good dad. His strong sense of responsibility. He wasn't crazy. His shifting feelings for her were normal. She'd gone from being his best friend to being something more.

His hand still on her stomach, he said, "Thank you for this."

Time stood still as they gazed at each other. Then she stood on her tiptoes and brushed her lips across his. The rightness of it tightened his chest. He couldn't imagine anything more perfect. It was a moment he'd remember his whole life. They were as connected as two human beings could be. The power of it sent desire and longing rising in his gut. They met and merged in an emotion so foreign he couldn't name it. He had never imagined a man could feel two incompatible things simultaneously, but here he was drowning in a happiness about parenting with her that seemed at odds with a burning male need.

"You're welcome." She took a breath and looked him in the eye again. "I've been thinking about this a little more than I let on."

"Oh, yeah? What did you come up with?"

"This might be the only time either one of us has a child. The one time either one of us will go through a pregnancy. I think it's sort of a shame to have only half the experience."

"Half the experience?"

"Marco, we're friends. We've *been* together. I think it's a little foolish to stand back and be all prudish when we could be experiencing something wonderful."

Just the thought of where this conversation was going made him swallow.

"It will be difficult enough when I go back to Rome and we're doing all this long distance. Why would we waste this time now when we could be enjoying it the way parents should?"

He licked his suddenly dry lips. She gave him a hopeful smile and he was lost. This wasn't just about sex or fun. It was the connection that got to him. He'd been longing for this since he'd first heard she was pregnant. He hadn't put her in his penthouse in the hope of getting accustomed to her. He'd wanted to share this. All of it.

He kissed her, longer and slower than how she'd kissed him. His heart expanded to the point when it might burst, so he stepped back.

"You're sure?"

"Marco, I'm not even sure why it took us so

long to figure out that we should be sharing this."

Her saying that made him laugh out loud. "Well, we're certainly adding a new dimension to our friendship."

Her hands reached for his shirt buttons. "Two if you think about it." She paused in unbuttoning his shirt. "No. Really only one. We want to have the full parenting experience. This is it."

Putting her hands under the shoulders of his shirt, she slid it back and it billowed away.

He didn't waste a second in evening the score. Except he didn't unbutton her pajama top. It was big enough that he could grab the hem and tug it over her head.

"Isn't that cheating?"

He would have laughed, but she wasn't wearing a bra and he'd revealed the beautiful breasts he remembered from their night together. He bent and nipped at them before running his tongue over the soft skin. He groaned. "Exactly as I remember."

She drew a deep breath that ended in a moan. "Me too."

He laughed, happier than he could ever remember being. With his hands floating down her naked back, he bent and kissed her deeply. Sensation rippled through him as pleasant anticipation grew into fiery need. The kiss leveled up to another dimension. His hands slid under the elastic waist of her pajama bottoms. Hers raced to his belt buckle.

Within seconds, they were flesh to flesh. Need drenched him in red-hot embers. He rolled her with him to his bed and indulged his hunger, allowing his hands to touch every inch of her. The feeling of her fingers streaming along his skin added fuel to the fire, nudging him to run his lips over her breasts and belly.

Desire roared through him, demanding release. He rolled her to her back and kissed her before joining them. The perfection of it nearly did him in, but he held on, taking her on a journey of sensation that rocked them both. It built and built until it exploded in a release that shook him to his core.

CHAPTER TEN

MARCO ROLLED AWAY from her and flopped to his pillow, breathing as heavily as a man who'd run a marathon.

Eleanora was right there with him. She couldn't seem to catch her breath as the energy of release and the boneless feeling of satisfaction took everything she owned.

"Okay. This was a good idea."

She glanced across the pillows with a smile. "Yes. It was. And kindly remember it was mine."

He laughed. "I had this idea long before you did. I simply wouldn't let it fully form in my brain because I didn't want to offend you. I wouldn't even let myself try to think a way to make it happen."

"You mean a good excuse to make it happen."

"Ms. DeLuca." He sat up. "Are you saying you used a ruse to get me into bed?"

"No. I meant what I said. We are about to be parents. There's a closeness to that. I want it."

He lay back down. "I do too." He paused for a second before adding, "I want it all."

"Diapers?"

He sat up and gaped at her. "Stop always jumping to the hard parts. Remember the low-hanging fruit theory?"

She sighed. "Figure out the easy things first so you get a feeling of accomplishment that will boost you into being able to do the more difficult stuff."

"Exactly."

"Meaning we're back to names?"

He lay down again and didn't answer for a second. When he did speak, it was carefully. "Since we've changed our definition of what we want, I think there are new avenues to finding solutions to the other things."

He confused her so much, this time she sat up and looked down at him. "What?"

He slid his hand to her bottom. "For instance, as long as we're having a relationship through the pregnancy, traveling to and from Rome for visits might show us some things we need to know about handling visitation."

"Oh." His hand on her so intimately distracted her enough that focused thought was difficult. Speaking required real effort. "You'd come to Rome to visit me?"

He nodded. "And as long as you were allowed

to travel over the next six months, I'd expect you to come to Manhattan to visit me."

She thought about that.

"I have a private plane at my disposal. *We* have a private plane at *our* disposal. Once you grow accustomed to that convenience, it might help you to understand how our child could easily travel to Manhattan for my scheduled visits."

"You would put an infant into an empty plane and fly him or her across the Atlantic and then scoop her up when she arrived?"

"No. Either I would fly to Rome to get her, or I'd send the nanny. In fact, I'm thinking sharing a nanny might make this work even easier."

"Huh." Her face scrunched as she considered it. "I see what you're saying."

"Okay, if you're able to consider that. Here's something else I'd like you to consider." He rolled her to her back and landed on top of her. "Stay with me. Here. Until January first."

Confusion had her face contorting again. "You want me to stay until after the holidays?"

"Yes. But think it through. You're already spending Thanksgiving so we can tell your parents, and you promised your mother you would have Christmas dinner with her and your dad. What I'm doing by asking you to stay is saving you who knows how many transatlantic flights."

She snorted. "You're so helpful."

"Yes," he said seriously. "I am."

She slapped his shoulder playfully, but when her hand landed on his solid skin, it lingered.

Their eyes met and he smiled at her before he lowered his head and kissed her. Every inch of her body warmed. Every nook and cranny of her heart filled with joy. And she wondered why she was arguing over a couple of trips when staying with him would be absolutely glorious.

She woke the next morning to find Marco staring at her. Her eyebrows rose but she said nothing.

He kissed her. "Good morning."

"Good morning." She waited half a second before she said, "What's up?"

"I was just wondering when we'll be able to feel the baby move."

The one consequence to involving Marco in every step of her pregnancy was the barrage of questions. It wasn't just that his curiosity was insatiable. It was more that he liked knowing absolutely everything about everything.

Luckily, she knew the answer to this. "About four months."

"And we're—"

"About three months along."

"Meaning, we'll feel the baby move around Christmas?"

She nodded.

He dropped a kiss on her mouth before he got out of bed. "All the more reason for you to stay through the holidays."

She laughed. "You can stop. I already decided it's probably a good idea. Though it wouldn't hurt for me to make an appearance or two in Rome. Maybe I fly there the Monday after Thanksgiving and around the fifteenth of December?"

"And stay a whole week each time?"

She shrugged. "How about only a day or two."

He said, "Okay," before he caught her hand, helped her out of bed and headed to the shower.

After making love in the shower and eating doughnuts for breakfast, Marco suggested they move her things from the guest bedroom to the primary suite before going Christmas shopping.

"I don't have a gift for my dad or my sister." He helped her carry her suitcase to his room. "Other years, I sent them flowers or candy or something easy like that. This year because we're getting together again, I think I need actual gifts."

"Definitely." She paused before asking, "Where'd you get the chocolates?"

"I had them shipped from Belgium…" He laughed. "You're hungry for chocolate?"

"You could have gotten chocolate icing on at least one of those doughnuts."

He brushed a kiss over her lips, then set her

suitcase on the small bench where she could either unpack it or have easy access to it. "I'll remember for next time."

"I think you should also get a box of the chocolates from Belgium."

He laughed and she unpacked, using two drawers he emptied for her and a small section where she hung her work clothes.

Skipping lunch, they headed out to Bloomingdale's then Saks Fifth Avenue. He couldn't find anything for his dad, but Eleanora helped him select a beautiful cashmere sweater for Chiara. She bought expensive pajamas for her mom but told Marco she'd be ordering tools for her dad.

"Small things so he can do some busywork around the house."

He thought of all the work that probably needed to be done in the family cabin, where his dad wanted to spend Christmas Eve. But he dismissed the worry. By Christmas his dad would have already done all that work. "Good idea."

On a whim they walked into a toy store. Marco glanced around in awe.

"We could get a crib with cartoon characters on it."

She laughed. "A mobile with characters would be smarter." She looked around too. "Are you going to go nuts buying things for this kid?"

"Maybe. Probably." He shrugged. "Who knows?"

She laughed at him, and he spent an hour looking at toys that their baby wouldn't be interested in for years. But she let him have the afternoon to think pleasant thoughts. He recognized it was because she wanted him in a positive frame of mind, so he'd stop researching possible complications. Still, a rest from overthinking was good. Thanksgiving he drove them to her parents' house in his Range Rover. They arrived at the two-story Colonial house after a leisurely drive. A light dusting of snow had fallen. To be on the safe side, he raced around the SUV's hood to open her door for her and help her out. He held her hand walking to the front door but when she pushed it open, he dropped her hand.

He wasn't entirely sure how the sexual side of their parental enjoyment worked, but he did know that it wouldn't be fair to give her mom and dad the wrong idea. He and Eleanora might be having a child together, but they were both on the same page about long-term relationships. He didn't believe in them. Hers hadn't worked out. They knew romantic relationships were temporary. Meaning, it would be wise to keep this one from her family.

"Mom! We're here!"

Her mom raced out of the kitchen drying her hands on a pumpkin-colored dish towel. Immediately, she hugged Eleanora, then Marco.

"I'm surprised you were free," she said to Marco as she pulled back from her hug.

"My family doesn't always do holidays."

Patty DeLuca gasped. "Then you should come here for more of them."

He laughed. "Thank you. But you'd get sick of seeing me."

"Nonsense. James! The kids are here."

Eleanora rolled her eyes when her mom referred to them as kids, but Marco wasn't surprised that was how her mother still saw them. From the time he was six and Eleanora was five, they had been as thick as thieves.

Her dad came out of the room to the right. Marco could see the big-screen TV and the football players currently occupying the screen. He hugged Eleanora, then shook Marco's hand.

"How's business?"

"Not the same since you retired."

James DeLuca owned the company that supplied linens for Grand York's restaurants and eventually the hotel bedrooms. He'd made a small fortune. Which was why he could afford a good-sized house in Connecticut.

"Oh, baloney," James said. "The people I employed didn't forget customer service just because I sold the company to somebody else."

"No," Marco agreed. "They haven't. It's still the best place to get our linens."

Her dad took their coats. While Eleanora helped her mom in the kitchen, Marco watched some of the game with her dad. A bowl of chips sat on the coffee table beside a bucket filled with bottled beer smothered in ice.

"Help yourself," James said.

Marco took a beer.

"So, anything new?"

"Having Christmas with my dad at the old cabin."

James sighed. "We had some good times at that cabin."

"We did."

"How is your dad?"

"Good." At least he was as far as Marco could tell from their phone conversations.

One of the teams scored and a roar erupted from the television. James cursed and his attention zoomed to the game and stayed there until Eleanora's mom came into the living room to get him to carve the turkey.

From there everything became a blur as Marco helped Eleanora put platters of food on the table, James carved the turkey and Patty supervised.

The turkey was perfect. The gravy tasted like a gift from the gods. The mashed potatoes melted in his mouth and the pie gave new meaning to perfection.

They talked about everything and nothing.

Marco kept waiting for Eleanora to deliver the good news, but she didn't mention her pregnancy.

When Patty rose to begin clearing the table, Marco stopped her. "Eleanora and I have something to tell you."

Eleanora's eyebrows rose. Patty sat again. "You do?"

"Yes."

Eleanora cleared her throat. "Yeah, Mom. Um. Marco and I are going to have a baby."

Patty clutched her chest. "That's wonderful!"

James rose to hug Eleanora, then clasp Marco's hand before enveloping him in a bear hug. "I am going to throw you two the wedding of the year."

When neither Eleanora nor Marco answered, the dining room fell silent.

Finally, Eleanora cleared her throat. "Marco and I aren't getting married."

James's gaze homed in on Marco. "What?"

"Well, sir, we're friends who sort of slipped up the night of the grand opening of Eleanora's hotel. We're not—" He glanced at Eleanora. "Together."

"The hell you aren't!" James pointed at Eleanora's stomach. "That baby says you are."

"No. Dad. We're not. We're two professional

people who love our jobs. Neither one of us has time for a committed relationship."

Patty frowned. "But you're going to have time for a baby?" Her disappointed expression intensified. "And you live in two different countries. How is that going to work?"

Marco took a seat, hoping everybody else would return to theirs. Eleanora did. Then her mom sat. But her dad stared at Marco for a good twenty seconds before he reluctantly returned to his chair.

"For one, we're going to share a nanny," Marco said. "She'll take care of the baby when he or she is with Eleanora." For the first time since he'd thought of it, Marco was totally grateful he and Eleanora had agreed to this. "Then she'll come with the baby when he is spending time with me."

Eleanora said, "She'll be a constant in the baby's life."

James snorted. "A nanny, not a parent, will be your baby's constant?"

The dining room grew quiet again and stayed that way.

After far too long without anyone talking, Patty suddenly took a breath and her face brightened. "You know what? I'm a firm believer that all things happen for a reason." She laughed shakily as her gaze drifted from Eleanora to Marco. "Something drew you together at that party in Rome. Maybe you should trust that instinct and give a relationship a try."

"Mom, you already said our biggest problem. I work in Rome. He works in Manhattan."

"Oh, poppycock," Patty said. "The man owns the company you work for. If he wanted to shuffle things around, he could."

"Not really, Patty." Marco winced. "There would be too much to change for me to work from Rome."

"And I can't work from Manhattan. I run the hotel *in* Rome. That's my baby."

"No. Your baby's in your tummy," Patty said.

James's expression turned thunderous. "Your sister has a job and three kids. And a husband." He caught Marco's gaze. "Someone who loves your sister enough to marry her so he can help her with *their* family."

Marco said nothing. At this point, he knew he wouldn't change anyone's mind, and he refused to bend under James's condemnation. He knew how bad things could become if they tried getting married and it didn't work. He knew how they'd hurt each other. He would not budge.

"Okay," Patty said, "I'm going to leave you two to just think about this for a few weeks before I say anything else. But trust me. Babies aren't easy. You're going to need each other."

"And we'll be there for each other," Eleanora assured her mom.

"No," James said. "*You'll* be there for him. Like you always are. He won't be there for you because he's never had to be. He spent his life giving you orders that you take. Even when you were kids taking the boat out, he'd be the captain and you'd be the first mate scrambling around doing everything he said." He shook his head. "Trust me. This is going to turn out just like that. With him giving orders and you doing all the heavy lifting."

Marco's mouth fell open. *Was that how they really saw him?*

Eleanora took a breath. "We'll work it out."

The room grew silent again. Eleanora rose. "How about if Marco and I do the dishes?"

James tossed his napkin to the table. "That won't prove he's going to do his share of the work with your child. It just proves he knows how to suck up." He stormed off to the living room again and Patty smiled shakily.

Eleanora shook her head. "I don't understand why you two are angry. You're getting a grandchild."

"Oh, we'll love another grandchild, and your dad will stop being mad. But right now, he and I both see that you're missing the obvious."

"Trust me, Mom. We'll think it through."

Patty smiled stiffly. "Well, I guess that's the best we can hope for."

She stood up and supervised the clearing of the table, packaging of leftovers and washing the dishes. By the time they were done, it was dark enough that Marco suggested they might want to head home.

Patty and James's hugs to Eleanora were stilted. But neither even attempted to hug Marco.

Weird feelings tumbled through him. The DeLucas were furious with him. But he could handle their criticism. It was Eleanora he was worried about. Did she also think that he was just a guy who gave her orders and she did all the work?

Was that how she saw them raising their child?

CHAPTER ELEVEN

MARCO OPENED ELEANORA'S door of the Range Rover. "That did not turn out like I'd expected."

As confused as he was, Eleanora climbed into the SUV. "That didn't turn out like I'd thought either. My parents aren't usually so far behind the times."

"Well, they aren't happy about us not getting married."

"Maybe they just need some time to adjust?"

"Maybe." He slammed the door closed, walked around the SUV and slid behind the steering wheel. For the first time since they'd arrived at the DeLucas', he glanced at his phone.

"Daniel sent an SOS text."

From working in the Manhattan office, Eleanora knew Daniel was the new manager for the original Grand York Hotel. He'd been assistant manager, so he knew the ropes. But he was a bit shaky about being totally in charge.

Marco glanced at Eleanora. "Mind if we stop there on our way home?"

"No. That'd be great. I love seeing that hotel."

He sniffed a laugh. "Me too."

"Your family's first venture into the world of hospitality." She smiled at him, hoping to return his focus to positive things. "And look how you've grown. You should be so proud."

"I am."

He said the words, but his heart wasn't in them. They made the almost two-hour drive back to Manhattan with Eleanora taking great pains to avoid the subject of her parents' reaction to her pregnancy. When she ran out of things to discuss about the Pearsons' wonderful business and her pride in the Grand York Rome, she jumped into questions about the new hotel in Paris: how far along the plans were, the exact location, other locations they had considered, who was designing the lobby.

If he noticed she was diverting his attention, he didn't let on. He happily discussed the new hotel until suddenly they were at the first Grand York.

A sedate but beautiful pale brick structure in the heart of Manhattan, it never failed to take her breath away. Some of the happiest moments of her life happened here. Especially the good fortune of having a guaranteed job while she was getting her degree.

After Marco parked the Range Rover, they walked into the lobby. Two reception desks sat parallel to each other. Skylights normally brought sunlight into the space but given that it was close to ten o'clock at night the lighting was subdued, except for the colored lights that twinkled on the twenty-foot Christmas tree that sat in the middle of everything. Open as it was, the lobby rose to the skylights displaying the open corridors of all the floors. Fresh evergreen boughs lined every railing, giving the lobby the scent of Christmas.

Eleanora soaked it all in. "It's beautiful."

"The staff always decorates on Thanksgiving," Marco said as he approached the first registration desk. "I understand Daniel's looking for me."

The young woman frowned. "Daniel's been gone since eight o'clock."

"He texted me at three," Marco said with a wince. "But I didn't read it until we started driving home from Connecticut." He smiled his thanks at the reception clerk, and he pulled his cell phone from his pocket to call Daniel.

Walking away from the reception desk, he said, "Hey. It's me. Sorry I took so long to get back to you. I was at dinner with Eleanora's family and didn't look at my phone."

Eleanora glanced around the lobby as he spoke. With the main lights dimmed—even the reception area had only desk lights—the area was dark, yet shiny. Or maybe the lack of light from the skylights exaggerated the sparkle of the multicolored bulbs on the tree and the reflection of lights off the tinsel.

Putting his phone back into his coat pocket, Marco walked over to where she stood by the tree. "Daniel had a question about the decorations. When he couldn't reach me, he made an executive decision."

She glanced at the tree. "Whatever decision he made it was the right one. The tree is beautiful."

"He hunted around until he found an old picture and decorated the tree to match that."

"Smart."

Marco sniffed a laugh. "He didn't want to make a mess of the lobby Christmas tree his first year as manager." He took a long breath. "It's just as I remember my mother decorating it. I'm glad he found the picture."

Eleanora suddenly realized why Daniel had panicked. This Grand York was the first hotel in the Pearsons' vast holdings. It was the one Marco's mom had put her stamp on. Especially at Christmastime.

"It's beautiful."

The reception area lights dimmed a bit more, until they were down to two desk lights. One for each clerk. Marco glanced at the two clerks working registration. "There must not be any late arrivals tonight."

"They're probably getting ready to settle in and study." Both clerks were young. Eleanora had seen the textbooks sitting beside their keyboards. She'd done the same thing while at university. She'd worked as one of the registration clerks and studied when the hotel got quiet at night.

Suddenly the music of a Christmas song drifted into the lobby. Slow and heartfelt, the melody surrounded them.

As if as surprised as she was, Marco glanced around, then he smiled, took her hand and lifted it so he could twirl her once.

She laughed nervously. "What are you doing?"

"Taking the edge off."

"The edge?"

"You have to admit it hasn't been our easiest day. The next few months will be difficult like this. And if your parents are right, having a baby's going to make our lives even crazier. I think we should enjoy every opportunity like this to relax."

He pulled her into his arms and danced her to a more private area behind the tree.

"Aren't you afraid the clerks will see, and rumors of this will get back to your dad?"

"What rumors? That we danced? We're friends. It's not like you're wearing a sign that says you're pregnant."

She laughed and shook her head, but she quickly grew serious again. "I know today was weird and I'm sorry. Had I known my parents would react so badly, I would have told them alone."

They danced a few more steps. "That's not our deal."

The nostalgic music, the lights of the tree and being held by Marco, all lulled her into a weird, surreal place where everything felt like magic. She could have happily nestled against him and forgotten the world, but she had to make sure Marco didn't go off the deep end with rules and deals and whose job was what.

"It's not our deal, but I'm trying to make this whole experience go as smoothly as possible."

He pulled her a little closer, danced a few more steps. "Maybe you shouldn't."

She pulled back so she could see his face. "Now that's just crazy talk."

"You can't always dictate how people react to things...how they feel. We're forming a team. A parenting team. Your mom and dad will catch on soon enough. When they do, it will show they respect us enough to trust what we're doing."

She thought about that, as the music lulled her back to the soft place, the place where she didn't care to think. She wanted to snuggle against his jacket, close her eyes and enjoy the moment. The lights were low. The Christmas tree was perfect. She did trust her parents to respect her enough to let her make her own choices. And she and Marco were talking like the good friends they'd always been.

"You're not falling asleep on me, are you?"

She laughed. "No. Just thinking."

"About?"

About how perfect this was. She couldn't tell him that. She didn't want to give him the impression she was making more out of this than he intended. But deep down, she worried that she was.

That wasn't their deal either.

Marco's soft voice broke the silence. "Looking at the tree, thinking of how my mom loved it, it just snuck up on me that I'll never get to tell her that I'm having a child. She'll never see our baby."

The sadness in his voice broke her heart.

Swallowing hard, she looked up at him. "I think mothers can see the future."

He snorted. "What?"

She wasn't 100 percent sure what she was

saying, wasn't even sure he wouldn't think she was a bit off her rocker, but she hated seeing him so sad and if sharing something helped, she would share.

"I think that when mothers look at their kids, they see who they are, what they're capable of and they see their future. I think when your mom looked at you, she saw you taking the reins of the Grand York Hotel Group from your dad and making sure his vision flourished."

He considered that for a second before he said, "Maybe."

"But I also think she knew you'd have children some day and if she didn't picture them exactly, she knew you'd take the best parts of what she taught you and the best of what your dad taught you, and the myriad things you learned other places and she knew, in her heart, that you'd give your child a hundred percent because that's how you do everything."

Tears filled Marco's eyes and he swallowed hard. Her dad's comments about him being a user had stung. Mixing that with the heavy sense of loss he felt looking at his mom's vision of a Christmas tree had shattered something in his soul. His life had been filled with very high highs and very low lows. Sometimes it was difficult to reconcile it all.

"You think that's what she saw?"

"Yes."

With his faith in the basic goodness of life teetering, he grabbed her words like a lifeline. He hoped that was what his mom had seen. His dedication. His commitment. His hard work. He couldn't imagine she'd seen him as a father, since he'd never seen himself that way. But if she had, Eleanora was correct. She'd have known he'd give parenting his all.

Deciding everything had gotten too real, he blinked away the tears brought on by memories and wishful thinking and teased her. "And how do you know, smarty-pants?"

"Because I'm starting to get those feelings now. Inklings of possibility. As if our baby's trying to show me who he or she wants to be. Once I get the full picture, I'll share it with you, then as parents we can show them the way to the vision we see in our heads."

It sounded a little like magic and hope rolled into one, but there was a comfort to it, like a bridge that connected what was with what he wished could be. "So, you think my mom saw me as a dad?"

"I think she saw you as a little bit of everything good and wonderful."

He knew she had. Though he knew she had seen the bad as well as the good, she'd witnessed his determination, if only because she'd put some of that fire to be the best in him.

They danced another few steps before Eleanora said, "Now that your two clerks think we're crazy, we should probably go home."

He broke away, but only far enough to take her hand and loop her under his arm again. If they hadn't danced, hadn't had this talk, he would have returned to the penthouse missing his mom because nowhere reminded him more of his mom than the Grand York at Christmas. But Eleanora had taken his sadness and turned it into hope, a little ray of light that cracked into the grief of loss and showed him a vision of his mother that made him smile.

He owed her for that. He owed her for a lot of things.

"They can't see us back here."

"But if they do there will be gossip."

He sighed and dropped her hand. "More gossip."

"Hey, people are curious, and that curiosity will grow when I start to show."

After talking about his mother, remembering her as he'd known her and getting a new vision of who she probably really was, talk of gossip sounded trivial. "I guess."

"We didn't do so hot at explaining ourselves to my parents today. So maybe we should work out a story for how to explain our situation to people who aren't related…like employees."

He slid his arm over her shoulder and walked her to the front of the Christmas tree. "Or maybe we shouldn't."

She didn't reply and he knew she wanted to hear his thoughts on telling their employees. He worried for a second that this was one of those things her dad meant when he'd intimated Marco called all the shots. But he might know Eleanora a little better than her parents did. She wanted his honest input so she could evaluate it. If she didn't like it, she'd argue. Just as his mother would have held her ground with his dad.

"Maybe we should let people think what they will think."

It's what his mother would have done. She'd have shaken her head and said, *"People will always talk. Doesn't matter."*

They walked through the lobby. Passing the reception desk, they said, "Good night."

The clerks looked up and smiled. "Good night."

When they reached the lobby exit, Marco turned and took one last look at the tree. He liked believing that his mother had seen into the future and known he'd do his part to fulfill his father's dreams. It gave him the sense that she was with him, even if it had only been through their imaginations.

Somehow it made it easier to think about spending Christmas with his family, not as a trio of people sharing a great loss, but as three people who recognized the impact she'd had on their lives and who were happy to have known her.

And he'd only gotten here because Eleanora shared an insight she might not have had if they hadn't created the child that lived inside her.

His connection to their child took a new meaning. Working through the ins and outs of being a parent, he understood his mom better. Understanding his mom better, he saw his position as a parent with a new depth of purpose.

He was also beginning to see Eleanora a little differently.

They returned to the penthouse and entered the main area to find Sunrise and Sunset asleep in their beds. He shrugged out of his coat, before he helped Eleanora with hers and tossed both onto an available chair. Then without a word, he took her hand and led her back to the primary bedroom.

He caught her by the elbows and pulled her close for a long, searing kiss.

He couldn't shake the feeling that everything

was connected. He'd needed something—a way to push past his lingering grief, or maybe his fear that grief would ruin his family's reunion—and she'd given it to him.

She'd connected the past to the future.

Unable to stop himself, he slid his hands to the bottom of her sweater and yanked it over her head, revealing the prettiest yellow bra he'd ever seen.

"You have spectacular underwear."

"Sweet talker."

He laughed but realized that maybe he could be better at that. Men liked visuals and tactile sensations—like pretty underwear and soft skin. Women liked words.

"Let's see if the panties match." With a quick unsnap of the closure of her jeans followed by a shove that puddled them at her ankles, her yellow panties were revealed.

"Very nice."

Kicking her jeans off her feet, she laughed. "You don't have to narrate."

He pulled her to him again, luxuriating in the feel of her softness against him. "What if I want to?"

"You want to narrate?"

The skepticism in her voice made him laugh. "I want to woo you."

She pulled back. "Really?"

"Oh, you don't think I can?"

"I just don't believe it's necessary for two people who know each other to—"

"Whisper the truth?" He divested himself of his clothes in as few movements as he had gotten rid of hers, then slid his mouth across the hollow of her throat, the place he knew wasn't merely soft; it was sensitive. His lips rode the curve of her jaw. "What crappy boyfriends you must have had."

She laughed breathlessly. "Yeah. They were the worst. But we've been over that."

"And there's no need to talk about anybody else when I have you here, so soft and pretty, right in front of me."

He watched her swallow hard and knew he was getting to her, knew wooing her was the right thing to do. Sliding his knee between her thighs, he gave her a light shove that landed them both on the bed, with her in a delightfully compromising position. He spent the next five minutes tasting every inch of her while describing her softness and his need for her. By the time, he was done her eyes were big, her breaths shallow. She was as soft as putty and so eager for him, he could have laughed at the control he had over her.

Except, naming every sensation he felt when he touched her, acknowledging every desire, had him as desperate as she was.

He joined them, gave action to the promises he'd made while wooing her and sent them both over the edge to oblivion.

CHAPTER TWELVE

ELEANORA STRUGGLED FOR BREATH. Not just because making love with Marco was always wonderful, but because of his words. He was right. Her other lovers really had been awful. The bar he set tonight would probably never be met by another man.

Lying beside him on the bed, she felt his love more clearly than if he'd said the words. But "I love you" were the three words he'd left out of an otherwise perfect wooing.

Her heart stumbled with longing to hear him say them. The need was so strong, she was tempted to have a conversation about their feelings, to tell him she loved him and tell him she could feel that he loved her too—

But, of course, he loved her. They'd been friends forever; they'd shared their childhoods, adolescence and now adulthood. If she told him she knew he loved her, he wouldn't deny it. He'd explain it. Then he'd explain again why that love wouldn't lead to anything more than friendship because he didn't want to hurt her—

The lines were getting blurred. In their effort to enjoy their pregnancy, she was getting bigger feelings for Marco than she'd ever had before. Even as he appeared to be handling everything logically, neutrally.

The next morning, she woke feeling more like her normal, commonsense self. Their situation wasn't about love; it was about the experience. It would last the length of her pregnancy. No more. His father had suffered horribly from the loss of his wife and regretted time spent working rather than being with her. Marco had seen that. And now he had the job his father had when his mom died. He would never make the same mistake his dad had.

Wishing he would—or he even could—wasn't merely wrong because she knew he wouldn't change his mind. It was also wrong because they'd made a deal. Wishing he would love her, say he loved her, wasn't fair.

After showering and putting on sweatpants and an oversize sweatshirt, she ambled into the kitchen, where Marco sat at the center island, eating a bagel.

He smiled at her and her stomach flipped. She finally realized that the problem wasn't fighting the need to get him to admit he loved her, but that she'd fallen even more in love with him than she had been at the grand opening celebration.

She loved him. Hopelessly. Desperately. Even though in their decision to enjoy the pregnancy, they'd made the deal that this part of their relationship would end when the baby came. She had to get her thinking back on track or she was going to come out of this hurt. Very hurt.

It was the one thing he didn't want and that she'd promised wouldn't happen.

"Can I make you a bagel?"

Shaking her head, she walked to the counter with the toaster. "I'll do it myself."

He turned on his stool. "Okay. While you're doing that, there's something we need to discuss."

She pressed her bagel into the toaster. "What's that?"

"We've done a great job of easing me into the pregnancy, making it so I feel a part of things. But that caused another problem."

Her heart and breathing stopped. Every wishful bone in her body came to attention. She knew what she'd felt from him the night before. Real love. The kind that didn't go away at the first sign of trouble or wear away as years took their toll.

He *loved* her.

Say it!

Let him say it!

"I still feel like you're doing all the heavy lifting."

She let her disappointment flow through her and pretended she felt it whoosh out through her toes and disappear into nothing. Given that they had an agreement, she had no right to be disappointed.

"You mean like carrying the baby?"

"I mean more like I should be pampering you."

"You could get me a chaise lounge where I can lie about all day while I'm being fanned and fed grapes by employees."

He laughed. So naturally. So innocently. So much like she would be able to laugh and enjoy their friendship if she hadn't fallen even more in love than she had been when they made their deal.

"More like I could bring you breakfast in bed."

"Our schedules don't allow that."

"Maybe I could order you those chocolates from Belgium."

"You were supposed to have already done that."

He frowned.

"Maybe it's better that you forgot." She faked a smile. "It's not good for me to gain too much weight."

He perked up. "How do you know? Did you

research that…?" His eyes widened. "Did you pick a doctor? Actually go to a doctor?"

"I've been with you more than without you. If I'd seen a doctor, you would know."

The toaster alerted her that her bagel was done. She set it on a plate on the counter and went to the refrigerator for cream cheese.

"What *is* happening with the doctor?"

"I've chosen one in Rome." That was sort of a lie. Actually, it was more of a prediction. She was sure she'd find a great doctor among the ones the emergency room doctor had listed for her. "In a few days I'll be in Rome. I'll see if I can get an appointment then."

"I should go too."

Oh, Lord no. She needed a few days away from him to get back her equilibrium about their relationship.

"First visits are fairly routine. Plus, if I don't like the doctor, I'll be moving on to another one. And another and another, until I find the doctor I like. That could get boring for you."

"I still think you need to find someone in Manhattan."

She thought about spending enough time with him that she needed a doctor in New York, and she knew she couldn't do it. While he enjoyed every step of their journey, she'd pine for him.

Yet, they'd promised to share the pregnancy,

take turns visiting each other. She couldn't break that promise. She simply needed to find a way to get a hold of her runaway emotions.

"Eventually, I probably should at least have a standby doctor in Manhattan. But that's a job for another day. Today, I'm working from here and making arrangements to be in Rome on Monday, leaving Sunday."

His head tilted as he thought about that. "Okay."

She breathed a sigh of relief that he didn't argue. After he left for the office, she did exactly as she said she would do. She made the obstetrician appointment with a doctor in Rome, video-conferenced with her staff and packed a bag for Italy.

Sunday night, she boarded the Pearson family jet and returned to Rome. Video calls were great, but luckily Marco understood that she needed to be at her hotel, with her staff. That meant she didn't have to risk him realizing that spending too much time with him was a bad idea because she was falling so deeply in love it was killing her. Or that her getting accustomed to having a jet at her disposal, two cats who adored her and a chauffeur were also bad ideas.

She was Eleanora DeLuca, ordinary woman. She could not forget that.

The days flew by. Her staff loved having her around. The visit to the obstetrician went well and before she knew it she found herself getting back onto the Pearson family jet.

With a heavy sigh, she settled into the seat. The smart play would be to sleep on the flight over and be ready for morning in Manhattan. But thoughts of Marco kept her awake. She'd missed him, pined for him. But they'd made a deal and she would keep up her end. No matter how difficult.

Worse, she got an unexpected picture of her son or daughter getting on this plane every weekend or every other weekend. Her child would be making this short, rushed trip every couple of weeks. While Eleanora would be standing on the tarmac, waving goodbye to her baby boy or girl.

She shook her head to dislodge the picture. As Marco had pointed out, they were lucky to have a private jet at their disposal. They'd also decided a shared nanny would make everything run smoothly.

Plus, she'd get time alone that she could use to get her work done, find a bigger condo, all the things she couldn't do with her child around.

A limo picked her up at the airport and took her to the penthouse. Jovial, happy-to-see-her Arnie wanted to help her with her suitcase, but she declined his offer, pointing out that it was a very small case.

He tipped his hat and let her go up to the penthouse alone. When the doors opened, Marco stood before her, a onesie with footballs printed all over it in one hand and a white onesie with a tulle ballerina skirt in the other.

She smiled and said, "Cute."

"I'm covering all the bases." He caught her hand, pulled her to him and kissed her soundly. "I missed you."

"I missed you too." She swallowed hard, knowing he had no idea of just how much she'd missed him. "But the trip showed me that I've been away from my hotel too much. I've gotta spend more time in Rome."

"If I remember correctly, we agreed to two trips this month." He helped her off with her coat. "And the rest of the time you're here until after the holidays."

"After the holidays?"

"You're spending Christmas with your parents and I'm spending the holiday with my dad and sister. After that we'll be splitting time between Rome and Manhattan."

She thought for a second.

He laughed. "The deal, remember? So that we can both enjoy the pregnancy, we'll split our time between Rome and Manhattan. You know. Some weekends I'll come visit you. Some you'll visit me. I also suspect you'll be having the baby in Rome because you can only fly until thirty-six weeks of pregnancy—unless you want to spend your last four weeks of pregnancy here?"

It wasn't exactly what they'd said or how they'd said it but that was spirit and intent of the agreement. A small light shined at the end of the tunnel. After the holidays, they'd have visits. She wouldn't be spending seven days a week with him. Only weekends.

She could absolutely handle that.

After hanging her coat, he led her to the sofa. He gently forced her to sit and took off her shoes.

"What are you doing?"

"I learned this while you were away. Remember how I said I feel like I should have more things to do?"

She cautiously said, "Yes."

"Well, I went online and did a deep dive, and this is one of the things I found." He began massaging her right foot. "Pregnant women like foot rubs."

The things he was doing to her foot sent a happy tingle through her. "All people like foot rubs."

"This is good, then? Something I can do for you?"

The earnestness in his voice went straight to her heart. It mixed with her relief that after the holiday she'd have more freedom and she relaxed. Now, instead of four and a half months of falling hopelessly in love, she only had a few more weeks. Once she was back in Rome, regardless of if she visited him or he visited her, she would have a home base and the end of their relationship would happen more naturally.

Meaning, she could allow herself to enjoy the foot rub. Enjoy him. For the rest of the month.

Marco ordered takeout and they ate dinner watching a movie. The distance he'd felt from her when she first arrived home seemed to have vanished, but his brain kept jumping back to the expression on her face when the elevator doors opened and she saw him.

He'd expected her to laugh at the onesies. Instead, she'd seemed unimpressed. That was when he noticed how tired she looked. He hated that she'd had to make two flights this month. Four, actually. Two to Rome. Two back to Manhattan. He'd tried to fix things with the foot rub, but instead of his mind focusing on her, it jumped to the realization that their child would be traveling like that most of his or her young life.

"You worry about the baby, don't you?"

She peered over at him. "Of course I do."

"And flying to Rome and then returning here didn't help."

"No."

"I guess we found a hole in our visitation plan."

"Maybe." She glanced at him again. "Probably."

"Okay. What are you thinking?"

"Honestly, Marco, I'm thinking it would be better for you to fly to Rome to see the baby until he's two."

He hadn't expected that, but after looking at the teeny-tiny clothes in the baby store, it was difficult to imagine forcing a baby to fly across an ocean once or twice a month.

"How often were we considering I'd see the baby?"

She shrugged. "What were you thinking?"

He thought of her mother's comment that he owned the company and how it would be easier for him to uproot than for her. But he couldn't uproot an entire corporate office full of people.

Still…

"What if I got a house in Rome?"

She blinked. "What?"

"What if I just bought a place? You could live there with the baby. I could visit."

"No." Her answer was immediate and firm. "Marco, we might be co-parenting, but there has to be room in our lives for each of us to actually have a life."

When the meaning of what she was saying

sunk in, he almost couldn't get his next question out of his mouth. His chest had tightened. His mouth went dry. But what she was insinuating was the truth of their lives. Something he'd insisted on. If he couldn't talk about it in the abstract, how in the hell would he ever live it in reality?

"You mean you want to date?"

She rolled her eyes. "Having a life is about more than dating, but yes. I'd probably want to date."

He ignored the searing pain in his chest. "My living in Rome, being able to take our child when you wanted to go out would actually help you."

She rose from the sofa with a sigh. "I'm sure all of this seems like fairy-tale fun to you. But you happily popping in to babysit is like a script for a sitcom. Except we don't have writers who will ensure everything ends up okay. Babies are a lot of work." Pacing the floor, she sighed again. "I know your heart's in the right place, and we're only in a planning phase. But trust me, you are not going to want to be my babysitter. You're probably not going to want to live in Rome. There'll be a flurry of love and excitement after the baby's born, but a few months in, we'll settle into a routine, and you'll get bored with us."

He tried to picture it. Tried to see her in a house, with a crying baby and him—well, he didn't know what he'd be doing. Would he be bug-eyed and confused, thinking it smarter to run than to help?

Was he really the guy her dad saw?

She bent down and kissed him. "I'm exhausted. I'm going to bed. I'll see you in the morning."

He watched her go, his entire body vibrating with something he couldn't explain. It wasn't just the vision he got of the confusion and noise of having a baby. It was that her dad wasn't the only one who anticipated he would bolt when the baby came. Obviously, she did too.

He expected to find her in his room when he went to bed two hours later. But she wasn't there. He assumed she was in the room he'd given her when she'd first arrived and settled onto his pillow telling himself that was fine. He was a bit annoyed with her for assuming the worst of him. But, forcing himself to think more positively, he also realized she was tired. She wanted the rest she would get alone in her own bed.

But his uncomfortable feelings about how she saw him wouldn't go away. He wanted to be part of their baby's life. He wanted to do a good job.

But she didn't think he could, and he couldn't create a scenario where he did.

Only because he hadn't been around a baby. He didn't know what to expect would happen, how the house would sound, what kind of schedule they'd have—

Still, he swore, somehow, he would ace this.

He wasn't one to shy away from a challenge. Let her dad think he would bolt. Let her assume the worst. He'd surprise everyone when he proved them wrong.

After a few minutes, his bed hadn't warmed up. It felt cold and empty. Lonely.

The real reasons she'd probably slept in another room filled him. If she wasn't angry with him, she was at least pulling away because their first real discussion about their child had gone poorly. She hadn't merely told him that he would probably leave her with the bulk of the work; she'd also told him she wanted time for herself—which he took to mean time to date. Now she was sleeping somewhere else.

He didn't get jealous. He could have, but he wouldn't let himself. The thoughts he was having weren't even confusing. They were straightforward truth. This, right here, right now—her sleeping in a different bed, their child's future a constant debate, his place in his child's life always up in the air—that was what his life was about to become.

His friendship with Eleanora began slipping away in his brain. He could see them at odds. He could see himself feeling left out of his own child's life.

He took a breath. Told himself not to think like that and reminded himself that he had an entire month to create the kind of connection between himself and Eleanora that was so tight she wouldn't lock him out or freeze him out— and he wouldn't leave her with all the hard work of raising a child.

But no matter how determined he was, he had no idea how they'd do either of those with her living in Rome and him living in Manhattan.

Tired of thinking about it, he sat up in bed. He had no clue where Chiara was, but he was tired of worrying about that too. He pulled his phone from the bedside table and called her.

To his complete surprise, she answered on the second ring.

"Hey, sis. Haven't heard from you. How're things in paradise?"

She went on to tease him about how happy she was and he relaxed, his frame of mind improving just from the sound of her voice. "Well, you'll be home in a few short weeks to tell us all about it."

Chiara didn't answer for a second, and Marco's trepidation about her coming to Vermont for Christmas Eve returned. But she eventually assured him she'd be there to give him all the juicy details. She surprised him by asking him to use his network of friends to investigate a computer whiz named Evan Kim. He agreed, thinking it would be better to put his mind on anything other than his current troubles. When they hung up the phone, he immediately began calling sources but it didn't take long to get the information she sought.

He called her back. She seemed happy with his report but she hung up quickly, as if she worried he'd ask why she'd wanted to know who Evan Kim was.

Marco stared at the phone. Talking to her was supposed to calm his fears about her not coming to the family Christmas celebration, but her questions about Evan Kim were odd and her inability to focus didn't help either.

Something was definitely going on with his sister. Knowing he'd never get to sleep, he picked up the remote and turned on his TV.

For as much as he wanted to confront Chiara about her secrecy, he couldn't. He didn't have any right to scold anyone about keeping secrets since he still hadn't told his family he was about to be a father.

But none of that mattered until he straightened things out with Eleanora, proved to her that he wouldn't desert her and their child.

CHAPTER THIRTEEN

MARCO WOKE IN such a good mood the next morning that Eleanora almost couldn't stand his chipper tone.

When she walked into the kitchen area, still wearing her pajamas, he grinned at her, raced around the center island and pulled her to him for a kiss.

She swore she was light-headed when he finally released her.

"I'm sorry."

She frowned. "For?"

"For some of the things I said last night. For whatever it was that made you sleep in your own bed."

"Exhaustion." She winced. "Honestly, Marco, I went to that room out of habit and just stayed there."

He laughed. "You were just confused?"

"And tired."

"All that stuff you said about me moving and visitation that was you being tired?"

"No. Most of it was the way I feel. We have to remember that our baby isn't a football we'll be tossing across the Atlantic. It's a tiny person." She took a breath. "And the one good idea we'd thought we'd come up with, actually means the nanny will be the constant in his or her life. We have to decide if that's what we want."

"For our baby to know the nanny better than he or she knows us?"

She nodded. "Exactly."

He fell to one of the chairs around the kitchen island.

"Don't let this overwhelm you." She caught his gaze so he could see her sincerity. "But really think about it. Even if it means you getting less time with the baby, wouldn't you rather have him or her know who their parents are, rather than being closer to the nanny?"

She could almost see that situation settling in his brain. As he thought through what she'd said, she helped herself to some breakfast. "It's weird for me to be eating breakfast."

He turned on the stool. "It's good for you to be eating breakfast."

She took her plate of scrambled eggs, fried ham and toast to the island and sat beside him. "I have to wonder if I'm making habits that I won't be able to break."

He sniffed a laugh. "You gaining weight is the least of our problems right now."

"Says the guy who isn't watching his careful eating plan go to hell in a fried ham sandwich."

He laughed and rose. "I've already said I wished I could be more involved. But there are some things I can't do."

"Yeah."

"Are you working from home today?"

"I shouldn't. I know the rumor about me being pregnant is all over Rome by now and it's probably bobbing around the corporate office."

"My executive staff brought it up at a board meeting. It's definitely bobbing around the corporate office."

"I should go into the office, looking not pregnant—"

"Not looking pregnant...yet," he reminded her. "People aren't dumb. When you start to show, they'll be doing the math in their heads. But right now, it's all just speculation."

She conceded that with a nod. "Staying home is the better idea, then. Plus, I seem to get so much more work done here."

"Then work from here."

"You can make all these decisions easily because you're the boss. I'm just a coworker to all these people who are talking about me being pregnant."

After a few seconds, he calmly said, "I never thought of it that way, but I see what you're saying."

"Maybe the best thing to do would be for you to tell your dad so we can break the news at the office. It might cause rampant rumors for a few weeks but then it would be over."

His calm cracked a little. She could tell he forced a smile. "Okay."

Her comment about breaking the news at the office followed Marco out of his penthouse and to work.

He'd barely had time to slip out of his overcoat before his personal phone rang. A quick glance at caller ID showed it was his dad. A video call no less.

"Hey, Dad!"

"Hey, Marco! Look at this."

His dad flipped the phone around to show him a quick visual of the cabin. "What do you think?"

The camera hadn't been on the cabin long enough for Marco to see if his dad was asking for Marco's thoughts on something he'd done or for his suggestions on what should be done.

"I don't know, Dad. I'm going to leave all cabin decisions up to you. Look, there's something I have to tell you—"

His dad's eyes widened. "What? What happened?"

The guy who had gone to the cabin to rest and get things ready went from happy and calm to panicked in the blink of an eye.

"Every year something happens to ruin our holiday." Joshua shook his head. "I honestly thought this year would be different."

"It will be."

"Then what's the crisis?"

"No crisis," Marco assured him. He took a beat to consider what would happen if he told his dad Eleanora was pregnant. A man who didn't have a grandchild should be thrilled at the possibility of getting one.

But the issue was Eleanora. Not getting married. Trying to raise a baby when they lived on different sides of the Atlantic. In that beat of time, he realized he had to have answers to these questions or his discussion with his dad might turn out no better than the discussion they'd had with the DeLucas.

Meaning, he couldn't tell the staff at the corporate office until they had answers enough that they could tell his dad.

He finished the call with his dad, emphatically promising him that he would be at the cabin the twenty-third because that was the one thing Joshua was holding on to.

Right now, he and Eleanora had to come to some concrete decisions for what would be the best for their baby. Once they did that, he was sure they could get her parents and his dad to look away from their dislike of Marco and Eleanora not getting married and to the fact that they were getting a grandchild. And not be concerned about the other issues involved, like who'd be traveling across the Atlantic.

Realizing how true that was, he relaxed. He and Eleanora would talk again that night and the next night and the next night, until they figured this out.

He returned to the penthouse after work ready to talk. Unfortunately, his phone rang before he even took off his coat. There was an issue in one of their West Coast hotels and he had to leave Manhattan for two days. When he finally returned, Eleanora had already left for Rome.

The feeling of being alone swept over him as he sat with Sunrise and Sunset eating dinner in front of the TV. He expected her to call—hoped for her to call—but she didn't. Even work seemed oddly empty. Which confused him so much that when his dad called again, he almost broached the subject of Eleanora being pregnant, but he remembered his plan. Until he and Eleanora knew what they were doing, he wouldn't tell his dad. He wouldn't tell anyone else. Instead, he listened to his dad ramble on about drywall and priming before painting.

When Eleanora returned the week before Christmas, he was so happy to see her that he grabbed her by the shoulders and kissed her soundly before wheeling her suitcase back to his room. He was not taking any chances on her mood tonight.

She laughed. "I wasn't going to go to the wrong room."

"Just a precaution," he said, trying to sound light and friendly.

"Well, I slept on the plane. I have my full thinking capacity and tons of energy."

He gave her a quick kiss. "Now that sounds promising."

"It is."

The smile in her eyes told him she had missed him as much as he missed her, and he reached another level of relief.

They ate a leisurely dinner, then made love in the shower and again when they finally went to bed.

A feeling of perfect peace settled over him. "I got a call from my dad today."

She raised herself to her elbow and smiled down at him. "You did?"

"Yeah. He's going nuts at the cabin. Fixing

things. Painting things. Showing me videos on my phone."

She laughed.

Suddenly, everything clicked back to normal with the two of them talking like the good friends that they were—

Of course, they weren't discussing custody or visitation or sharing a nanny—

He stopped his thoughts. He had to. He'd been so damned lonely for her while he was gone, then while she was gone that he'd come to an important conclusion. If all the time he'd get with her were the months until she had the baby, he wanted them to be perfect. They would decide some broad and general things now so he could tell his dad. Then they could argue and fight out the things that popped up after the baby was born—

But that was really the point. He wanted to remember—and he wanted *her* to remember—that they liked each other and were a team. The best way to do that would be to *be* a team for the last week they had together.

Right at this moment, with her nestled against him, calm and content, they were a team who liked each other.

This was what he had to keep—this mood, this sense of cooperation and liking each other and *trusting* each other. Good friends that they were, they *should* make wonderful parents.

They fell asleep spooned together. His vow of keeping their closeness intact, even after the baby was born, no matter what he had to do, ran through his brain as if on an endless loop. He did not want to say or do anything wrong.

His conviction shook a bit on Saturday when she went Christmas shopping alone. Sunday, she walked out of her bedroom dressed in joggers and told him she was going for a walk. He expected her to take the cats. Instead, she went alone.

After the elevator doors closed behind her, he cursed. "How the hell am I supposed to prove to her that we're a team when she never stays home?"

Sunrise and Sunset looked at him.

"Hey, she's the one being weird, not me."

Both cats stared at him, condemningly.

He sighed. "Okay, let's think this through. Let's figure out how to get her to warm up again." He thought for a second, then said, "She'd come out of her bedroom dressed for her walk. She hadn't had breakfast." He snapped his fingers. "I'll make breakfast. I'll have everything ready but the eggs when she gets back."

Sunrise tilted his head as if he thought any idea that involved food was sound. Sunset rose and trotted back to his sunny spot on the floor by the window.

Regardless of what Sunset thought, Marco gathered the things he would need to make breakfast, but he stopped. Her favorite food was toasted cheese sandwiches. He would make toasted cheese sandwiches for breakfast. That would make her laugh and make her happy. Hopefully, it would also dissolve whatever reason she had for always putting distance between them.

Feeling like the smartest guy on the planet, he buttered bread, grated cheese—for easier melting—and was ready when the elevator bell signaled she was back.

She walked out of the elevator pulling her gloves from her fingers and her knit cap off her head.

"How was your walk?"

"Freezing! We might not have snow for Christmas but it sure as hell is cold enough that we could."

"How about a nice warm toasted cheese sandwich?"

She looked at him for a second, then joyfully said, "I'm not hungry."

She sounded so relieved he would have laughed had she not spoiled his romantic gesture.

"Oh, thank heaven! I feel like my stomach is returning to normal."

He eyed the grated cheese and buttered bread. "That's great."

She finally saw that he'd already started the process. "I'm sorry. I didn't mean to mess up your plans. You can still make a sandwich for yourself."

"Or we could eat them for lunch."

She winced. "I have plans."

Words failed him. It was the last thing he'd expected she'd say. But why wouldn't she have plans? She'd gone from being a penthouse home-body to someone who raced out every chance she got.

Something had to be wrong.

Really wrong.

"One of my friends is coming into town to shop. We're going to grab lunch."

He pulled away from the kitchen island. He was going to have to do more than make her a sandwich to bring her back around. Except she didn't seem angry with him or even upset. She actually seemed happy.

"Okay. Enjoy your lunch."

She smiled. "Are you sure?"

"Yeah. Yeah." He batted his hand. "I wanted to get some work done this morning anyway."

"Okay."

She walked back to the bedroom.

He suddenly considered joining her, maybe tempting her into making love so she could remember that she liked his company, but he was back to being miffed at her. Why? Because she was happy? He wasn't that shallow.

Because she was happy without him? Again. Not that shallow.

Because she was clearly picking up her old life, looking forward to making a new life—without him—

Yes. That was the winner.

He stalked to the office, where he brooded instead of working. Around eleven, she opened the door and poked her head inside the room.

"I'm leaving now."

He forced a smile. "Have a good time."

"I will!"

Okay. They were going to have to talk. For real. Unfortunately, he had no idea what to say. He had no right to stop her from having a life.

Eleanora left the penthouse and stopped in the middle of the sidewalk, looking both ways to see if she could find her rideshare. She spotted it and got inside.

The driver, a young woman with yellow braids and a bright smile, put the car in gear and took off. After a few seconds she said, "I'm Mandy."

Eleanora smiled. "I'm Eleanora."

"Going shopping?"

"No. Having lunch with a friend who is going shopping."

"That sounds fun."

It sounded like a desperate woman, faking fun to Eleanora, but she kept her smile in place. "Thanks."

They reached the restaurant where Eleanora met her friend. Bootsie Montgomery had become a nurse and married a man who owned a plumbing business. They were the normal, average couple that Eleanora had always aspired being part of. Instead, she had become an executive, gotten pregnant with a man who didn't believe in marriage and now had plans to turn herself into a woman who raised her child alone, had passionate but brief affairs and traveled.

It would have been perfect if she hadn't fallen madly in love with Marco.

Particularly since she'd have to pretend that she liked him, as a friend, while she tried to fall out of love with him, as they raised a child together.

Sure. Piece of cake.

She returned home to find him sitting on the sofa with the cats. Sunrise was on the back of the couch, rolled in a ball behind Marco's neck. Sunset slept on his lap.

She suddenly envisioned him ten years from now, working Sunday, and sitting with his cats watching a movie to relax.

At least her future had travel and passionate affairs in it.

Of course, if she wasn't here right now, pregnant with his child, who knew? Maybe he'd be having a passionate but brief affair?

The image didn't cheer her. She went back to envisioning him as a forty-two-year-old bachelor who lived with his cats.

"How was lunch?"

"Great. Bootsie is still Bootsie."

He laughed as he rose from the sofa. "Come here. Let's talk."

"Actually, I'm kind of tired."

"Okay. Get a nap. We'll talk after. I know, while you nap, I'll look at take-out menus and get us a great dinner, and we'll talk while we eat."

"Marco, I had a big lunch. I probably won't even want dinner." She motioned down the hall. "And I'm at the good part of my book. I think I'm just going to read."

She walked back down the hall and he heard his bedroom door close. He took a second to appreciate that she was still in his room, but it didn't stop that weird feeling that bubbled up.

They hadn't had a real conversation since she'd

told him how she pictured his involvement after their baby was born— No. They hadn't had a real conversation since she'd basically admitted she expected him to bolt.

Here he was, trying to fix things, to show her that he might be a busy executive, but he intended to be a good father, and she wasn't giving him the time to do it.

He made the toasted cheese sandwiches that he'd started that morning and they were delicious. He had a moment of pure happiness even if she'd refused to enjoy the best sandwiches he'd ever made, but it didn't last long.

He liked her. She liked him. Their relationship wasn't supposed to go through dips and valleys like this. They understood each other.

At least he'd always thought they did. Until her dad made his comment about him giving orders and Eleanora doing all the work.

A hockey game came on and he and his boys sat on the sofa to watch it. Others might say the cats didn't actually watch the game, but they seemed to like the action as their eyes darted right and left following the players on the ice.

His team won and he swore Sunset wanted to high-five. His world felt righted until he went in the bedroom and found Eleanora sleeping. She'd once laughed about him sitting by the bed, watching her all night. But as he walked to her side of the bed and sat on the mattress at her hip, he realized he could do that.

With her face nestled into the pillow and her pretty red-brown hair billowing around her on the white case, she looked absolutely content and peaceful, as she rested. He thought about the difficulties of pregnancy, her tiredness, her desire to eat, the uncertainty of her future, and again he felt distanced from it all. Left out.

He thought about when she returned to Rome January 1. She'd be alone. He'd be alone. Their baby would be raised in a never-ending sea of two different houses, two different sets of family friends, two different cultures. The child of people who loved each other but were at odds.

Sitting beside her in the silent bedroom of his silent house, he knew that was the part that wasn't right. Making love the night of the grand opening had been perfect. Discovering she was pregnant had been shocking but now seemed—as she had said—like their logical next step.

Not being able to come up with custody or visitation terms, not liking the idea of his child bouncing between two continents, not liking the fact that their living arrangements *did* give him a way to skip out on the important things of raising their child?

Those were the things that felt wrong.

An arrangement like this might work out perfectly well for two other people, but he and Eleanora weren't two other people. They were Marco and Eleanora, best friends, who *wanted* to do things together.

The truth hit him then.

They *wanted* to do this *together*! She involved him every way she could. If she bailed on spending time with him, had lunch with a friend, it had nothing to do with their pregnancy. Nothing to do with their baby. In the end, anything, any decision that had to do with their baby, she involved him.

Because they *wanted* to raise this baby together.

And they should.

CHAPTER FOURTEEN

WITH EVERYTHING SO clear to him, Marco left the bedroom, found his personal phone and hit the contact button for the family jeweler.

Dex was surprised to hear from him. "What's up? Forget a date and need to apologize?"

Realizing it was nearly midnight, Marco laughed. "No. And that won't ever be happening again. I'm sorry for the late call, but I need an engagement ring."

The dead silence from Dex made Marco laugh. "I'm serious."

"Well, I'll be damned."

"Probably. But I'd like to come over tomorrow afternoon and see your prettiest rings."

"Any price I need to stick to?"

Marco named a number and Dex snorted. "In other words, there's no limit."

"Just get the rings ready. I'll be over after lunch."

One o'clock on Monday, Marco walked the three blocks to Dex's private showroom in snow that was wispy and cold. He brushed the annoying flakes off his shoulders as Dex greeted him.

A short round guy with thick black hair that seemed to blend with his big, mountain man beard, Dex came out from behind the counter to shake Marco's hand. "I could have come to you."

"Too risky. The past few weeks I've been learning just how much our staff talks."

"You thought they didn't?"

"I can be naive about some things."

Dex laughed and took Marco's coat. He handed it to a young clerk who scampered away with it. Dex led him to a small glass table sitting in a private corner. As Marco sat, Dex pulled a small velvet tray from the drawer below and set it on the table.

Diamonds winked at him. "Tell me what I'm looking at because I'm not really good with things like this."

Dex pointed to the first row. "These are three carats. Good sized but discreet."

He picked up the first one. "I think Eleanora would like something discreet."

Dex smiled. "Here's another selling point. I designed all six of these myself. I created them to be exclusive."

As he spoke, one of the rings suddenly stood out from the crowd. The band was thick, and the diamonds were a sideways eight, the symbol for infinity.

"I don't know much about jewelry, but I think this one sums up our relationship."

Dex inclined his head. "Interesting choice. Particularly since it's designed to be both the engagement ring and can be worn as a wedding band."

"I don't know why but that makes me like it even better."

Dex sat back. "Sometimes buying a ring is all about instinct. If this one is the one that calls to you, I'd say it's the one you instinctively believe she will love."

"I do."

Rising, Dex batted a hand. "Save your 'I dos' for the ceremony." He laughed at his own joke, then motioned for Marco to join him again at the counter.

Twenty minutes later he walked out with the ring box securely in his jacket pocket.

With Eleanora working from home again, he got out his phone and smiled. He was about to make a date with her. A date. It seemed silly to be so excited, but suddenly he realized how much they'd missed. How much they'd gotten backward.

She answered quickly. "What's up, Marco?"

"I'm calling to ask you to dinner."

"Oh."

* * *

Eleanora could have refused him. Maybe she should have refused him. But since their bad discussion about what would really happen after the baby was born, she'd put a lot of distance between them. Maybe too much.

She'd pushed him to see reality and she was pretty sure he had. Now, she could soften a bit so they could discuss their baby like two logical human beings.

"I'd love to go to dinner tonight."

"Good. Wear your best dress. This is going to be special."

Knowing how he liked making an event out of every little thing, she shook her head. "Okay."

That night, Eleanora dressed in the best dress she'd brought to Manhattan. She saw this dinner was his way of trying to get their friendship back to its usual good place. As close as it was to December 23—when he'd be leaving for Vermont and she'd be on her way to Connecticut to visit her parents—the day she'd deemed the official end of their romantic relationship—she decided to go along with whatever he wanted.

It also wouldn't hurt to get them back to the place where they were comfortable with each other. They might be on the same page about sharing a nanny, but visitation was back to being up in the air. Truthfully, that hiccup had shown her that they couldn't plan everything. Most things would be decided by whatever was going on in their lives. Their baby could get sick or be teething or potty training on weeks Marco was supposed to have him or her.

A shared nanny would alleviate a lot of that, but Eleanora would never force a sick child to fly across the Atlantic.

Childrearing on two continents would be a constant negotiation.

Not a fight. Not a battle. A negotiation. And she couldn't enter that phase angry with him for not loving her or avoiding him so she could stop herself from loving him. She had to get them back to normal now.

She waited for Marco to come home, getting annoyed that the later it got the longer she had to wait for dinner, but ten minutes before she might have called him her phone pinged with a text. Sam was downstairs waiting for her. Marco had told Sam to drive her to the restaurant.

Which was another thing. She would have to gently remind him that he couldn't pull these kinds of stunts with their child. And she needed to be calm and collected for the conversation they were about to have.

Annoyed with him, she suddenly wondered if it was wise to continue their relationship until the baby was born. Maybe a few weeks of closeness was all they'd get because trying to have a relationship might actually be getting in the way of making good decisions.

Her heart pinged, but she ignored it, slipping into her black wool coat and riding the elevator to the lobby.

"Well, would you look at you!" Arnie grinned at her. "All gussied up."

"I don't know about gussied." She glanced down at her black-and-white dress that did the best job of hiding her swollen stomach. "But I did clean up."

Racing to get the door for her, Arnie laughed. "You crack me up."

She smiled as he handed her off to Sam, who opened the limo door for her.

"Evening, ma'am."

"Evening, Sam."

"Going to a pretty fancy restaurant tonight. Big date?"

She downplayed the situation. For all Sam knew, they were friends sharing his penthouse while she worked at the corporate office. She wouldn't give credence to any gossip. "It gets boring sitting in the penthouse all the time."

Sam laughed. "That's something I wouldn't mind discovering for myself."

She slid into the car and took long, slow breaths to calm herself as they drove twenty minutes to a restaurant in a part of town she'd never seen. She couldn't believe she'd missed the obvious. While sharing the beginning part of the pregnancy had been joyful and wonderful, now that they had gotten down to the nitty-gritty of custody and visitation, their relationship was getting in the way.

Sam opened the limo door, then escorted her to the restaurant door, which he also opened. She walked into the quaint Italian place only to discover it was empty.

Just when she might have gone looking for a hostess or maître d', an older gentleman approached her.

"Good evening, Ms. DeLuca."

She smiled. "Good evening."

He motioned for her to follow him. "This way."

All the tables were dark, except for one in the back that was lit by a fat candle. Marco stepped into the glow of the small light and pulled out her chair for her.

She glanced up at him as she sat. "What's this?"

He took his seat. "Privacy."

"I know the gossip is getting to us, but—"

"I didn't want privacy because of the gossip. I wanted privacy for us."

She took a breath. "You closed down an entire restaurant so we could argue?"

"First, I own this restaurant. I'm allowed to take liberties."

She glanced around. "Your family owns this?"

"I own it. I have several investments."

"Oh."

"And we're not going to argue."

"We're not?"

A waiter brought small dishes of olives and cheese with two glasses filled with clear bubbly liquid.

Marco lifted his glass. "Sparkling water."

She nodded, then took a long swallow, grateful for the drink. Before she even reached for an olive, the waiter returned with a platter of salami and mortadella, served with cheeses and crusty bread.

She recognized it. She'd spent enough time in Italy to know the popular seven-course meal. "Are we having a seven-course dinner?"

"I wanted you to have a little taste of home." He smiled. "Your home in Rome."

He clearly hated that they'd fought, and she took the lovely meal as a genuine apology.

"So good," she said as she ate a piece of salami with the crusty bread.

"Don't fill up," Marco said. "That's two courses. We have five more, counting dessert."

The gesture and his good mood revived her hope that they could work out their child custody troubles, even if she was absolutely sure they needed to end their personal relationship.

Lasagna arrived next. Eleanora's stomach seemed to sigh with happiness.

He asked about her day, and she gave him a quick rundown, keeping everything light and positive. Then she asked about his day, recognizing that they were building a bridge or maybe rebuilding their good feelings for one another so raising their child couldn't be a constant battle.

Lamb arrived next, followed by the contorni, vegetables, and then the sorbet as a palate cleanser. By the time the salad arrived, Eleanora put up her hand. "I love to eat as much as the next person, but I think I've had enough."

He laughed. "You're not going to have dessert?"

"I'm stuffed. I can't eat the salad or cheese and fruit. Though I wouldn't mind having them wrap up our dessert for morning."

With a quick motion of his hand, he caught the attention of the maître d' and the short man raced over. "Everything was wonderful, but we're done." He smiled. "Although we would like dessert to go."

"Absolutely." He shuffled away, into the kitchen.

Marco took a long, slow breath. One of those breaths a person takes before they make a big announcement.

Eleanora's heart jerked to a stop. What if this dinner wasn't about making peace? What if he'd made some decisions without her and he was about to burst her bubble that they could co-parent by doing something heavy-handed like filing for custody?

She told herself Marco wasn't that kind of guy, then she looked around at the restaurant he *owned*. She'd thought there were no secrets between them, but clearly she didn't know everything about him.

Before she could say anything, he rose from his seat. Reaching into his jacket pocket, he went down on one knee.

This time when her heart stopped, she wasn't sure she would get it beating again. He was *proposing*?

"Eleanora, we've been dancing around this for weeks. Even your parents could see we love each other." He opened the box. "Will you marry me?"

She pressed her hand to her mouth. Every cell

in her body wanted to say, "Yes!" She longed to spring out of her chair, hug him to her and accept the ring—

No. What she really longed for was for this proposal to be real.

No. That wasn't it either. The proposal was real. Marco wouldn't do something like ask her to marry him if he didn't mean it. The problem was this wasn't the proposal of a man so in love he yearned to be with her. What she wasn't feeling from him or hearing in his voice was giddy romantic love.

The proposal was more of a duty—or an answer to a problem.

Her brain awoke. His reason for asking her to marry him came to her slowly. They'd had a blowout fight about custody, and Marco Pearson, smartest businessman she knew, pondered this from the vantage point of a work problem and he came up with the solution that solved everything.

They would get married.

She removed her hand from her mouth and swallowed hard. The ring winked up at her, surprising her with its beauty and meaning.

"It's the infinity symbol."

He smiled. "We have already been together

most of our lives. This just carries us into the future."

She wished he'd said he adored her, couldn't live without her, saw them growing old together. He'd said things like those when he made love to her. But that was different, just for fun, throw-away words. When it came to the future, he didn't think in giddy, happy terms. His mother's death had introduced him to some harsh realities of life. The way his father had mourned—still mourned—had taught him to be careful, cautious, to always hold a piece of himself back.

"I'm not getting a good feeling here."

She glanced at him, blinking back the tears that gathered on her eyelids. "Oh, Marco. I wish I could say yes. But we had our biggest fight over custody a few weeks ago. Our baby's not even born, and we can't make solid plans because in a lot of ways neither one of us can budge."

She pulled in a breath and rose from her seat. "So, your business brain decided getting married was the answer."

Her chest hurt so much from the urge to weep that she almost couldn't speak. But she had to get this out. "I might not ever find a once-in-a-lifetime love. But I don't want to be nothing more than the answer to a problem."

She shoved her chair back so she could walk

around the other side of the table and race out of the restaurant. Knowing Marco would follow her, she quickly told Sam she would be finding her own way back to the penthouse and ran up the street.

But Marco was faster than she'd thought. Her coat over his arm, he caught her before she even reached the corner.

Motioning for her to turn around so he could help her with her coat, practical, pragmatic Marco said, "Where are you going?"

"Back to Rome."

He took a breath. "Look, I know how I asked you to marry me wasn't very—"

"The problem wasn't what it wasn't. It's what it was. Insulting."

He put his arm around her. "You're shaking."

"It was pretty damned cold out here without a coat."

"Yeah. Let's go back to the penthouse and talk some more."

Her sound reasoning began to desert her. When she thought as pragmatically as Marco, she'd realized they needed to part. His offering her a ring out of practicality hurt. But with his arm around her and the voice of her friend suggesting they go back to the penthouse, everything inside her melted. But that was the problem. She loved him enough that she always gave him the benefit of the doubt, always enjoyed being around him. Driving to this dinner, she'd known they needed to separate. That was why she'd so easily seen the truth in his proposal. She'd been with him enough that when she separated her wishes from the truth, pragmatic Marco remained.

She didn't want to hear his reasoning. She didn't want to give herself the chance to read more into what he said than what he meant.

"You know what, Marco? Lately it seems we get ourselves into really big trouble when we talk."

"Okay. How about if we go back to the condo and rest?"

She nodded. He walked her back to the car and Sam silently opened the door.

After they were settled, Sam pulled onto the street.

Marco quietly said, "For the record, I didn't ask you to marry me because of the baby."

She shook her head. "Now's not the time."

"Is it so farfetched to think I could love you?"

She gaped at him. "It hasn't even been a month since you told me you'll never be all in in a relationship. *That's* not love."

He'd surprised her so much that she'd told

him the truth. It hung in the air like a demon ready to strike.

But she wouldn't take it back. She couldn't take it back.

CHAPTER FIFTEEN

CONFUSED AND DISAPPOINTED, Marco leaned back on the limo seat. He didn't say anything else to Eleanora through the drive to the penthouse. When they got out of the elevator, the cats raced to meet them.

"I forgot to text Wisdom!"

Eleanora removed an earring. "You're just a few hours late with their dinner. They're fine."

The cats looked at her as if she'd ruined their favorite toy.

Marco would have laughed but he could see she was tired and hurt.

The fact that he was the one who had hurt her by asking her to marry him, confused him so much he had no idea what to say or do. But he did realize her going to bed so they could discuss this in the morning was a good idea.

But she wasn't in a talking mood the next morning either. The irony of it perplexed him so much he couldn't think. He took the cats out for a walk, letting the fresh air give him perspective.

He loved her and wanted to marry her. But he'd made it clear to her that he didn't ever want to get married and that he didn't even want to be in love. So now that he loved her, she didn't believe him.

What he needed to do was woo her. As Sunrise and Sunset trotted along, he realized he'd done that. He'd wooed her so sweetly and sexily one night he'd about driven *himself* crazy—

But he'd done that while they were under the umbrella of their "deal." When they were just having fun. No strings attached. Nothing serious.

No wonder she didn't believe him. He'd shown her he could be a romantic while under the umbrella of a deal he'd made because he believed he would never love anybody.

To her, his marriage proposal had probably stunk to high heaven.

He let the cats trot along, wondering if he should try another proposal. Sure, the dinner had been nice. But because he'd been nervous, he'd kept everything simple. Maybe what he needed was a grand gesture?

He and the cats walked some more as he tried to decide on a grand gesture. It was too cold for a hot-air balloon. It was too close to Christmas to take her to Cabo San Lucas.

He could hire a mariachi band and make it light and fun. Or he could find a first-edition copy of her favorite book and say something serious and touching—

He stopped dead in his tracks. The cats stopped with a jerk and gave him a look. "Sorry, guys. I think I figured out what I did wrong." He turned to the right, went into a coffee shop. A few people eyed Sunrise and Sunset disapprovingly. He smiled apologetically, got a cup of coffee and quickly removed his cats from the premises.

When they reached the park, he sat on a bench, tied the cats' leashes to a tree beside it and sipped his coffee.

The cats looked at him. "I can't do something over the top like a hot-air balloon ride. That's meaningless. I have to think of something romantic to say. The problem is I used all my best lines the night I seduced her."

Sunset looked away, distracted by a leaf blowing in the light breeze.

Sunrise still gave him his full attention.

"I don't want to be repeating lines. I also need to go in a more romantic direction than…well…" He winced. "You know. Seductive."

An old man passed as he said *seductive*. He

turned and gave Marco a curious look. Marco saluted him with his coffee.

"You know what? We're far enough away from the penthouse that I can think about this as we walk back." He unwrapped the cats' leashes and started them in the direction of his building.

As they happily trotted along, he drank his coffee but nothing appropriate came to him.

But one thought did surface and take hold. If he didn't figure all this out before she returned to Rome, there'd be nothing to figure out. She'd be on her home turf. She'd take care of herself. She'd make plans without him.

His heart stumbled. He had until he left for Vermont to figure this out and he sure as hell hoped his brain came up with better ideas for proposing soon or he was going to lose her.

Eleanora took advantage of the time Marco was outside with the cats to repack her suitcase. She'd slept in her original room the night before and would continue sleeping there. She needed to get her clothes and toiletries out of the primary bedroom suite.

She was no longer confused. It might not have been a mistake that she and Marco slept together the night of the grand opening—it had actually been wonderful—but trying to fix something questionable with a bungled attempt at sharing her pregnancy had been wrong.

She should have realized she was too emotionally invested to share the pregnancy with Marco. She should have realized that pretending to be on the same page emotionally was a trap. But she hadn't. The day before, though, her thinking had cleared.

For as much as she ached for him to love her, he didn't. His proposal proved that. A man who truly loved a woman and was handing her a beautiful, symbolic ring, would have had love shining in his eyes and joy in his voice.

Technically, *she'd* put him in this awkward position. He liked her enough and wanted to be involved in their child's life enough that he'd begun imagining he wanted things that he didn't.

She had to set him free, go back to being smart, savvy Eleanora who knew the right things to do. No matter how much it hurt.

As she rolled her suitcase up the hall to her original room, she wondered why she was staying. She'd seen her parents at Thanksgiving, and they were still a bit miffed at her. More at Marco. But her too. Christmas would be stilted at best. Plus, her sister was coming home with her kids for Christmas. If she went to her parents' house, her dad would probably go off on another one of his tangents about her not getting married, and everybody's holiday would be ruined.

If she kept walking up this hall, to the elevator, down to the street, she could get a cab and be at the airport in a little over an hour. Once there, all she had to do was find a flight and she could be in Rome tomorrow.

Marco returned to the penthouse to find Eleanora had gone. At first, he considered she'd simply moved back into the bedroom she'd been using when she first arrived, but her suitcase wasn't there either.

He plopped on the sofa, ran his hands down his face and tried to ignore the two cats giving him a condemning glare. "It's not like I fired Wisdom. She's the one who feeds you."

The glares got worse.

He took a breath. "You know... Eleanora might have gone to her parents'." Sunrise perked up. "She was staying so she could spend Christmas with them. It's a few days early but if she's angry enough with me—" *Insulted. The word she'd used was* insulted. "Then maybe we just need a break."

Unimpressed, Sunrise sleekly trotted away. Sunset jumped up on the sofa and curled into a ball for a nap.

The quiet and cold feeling returned to his penthouse. His cats, two fairly amusing felines, didn't seem like the good company they usually were. He could do some work, but he didn't feel like that either. His job had shifted from being interesting and energizing to being just stuff.

He pulled in a breath at that thought. The Grand York was not just *stuff*. It was who he was.

Really? He was his job? A glorified bean counter?

Not liking his train of thought, he picked up his phone and called Eleanora's parents. He mentioned that she'd gone without finishing a discussion on something important and her mother said, "No. She's not here and she didn't call to say she was coming, but if she comes, I'll have her call you."

"Good. Good," Marco said, simultaneously tongue-tied and foolish. Her parents were not his allies. Even if he told them he wanted to marry their daughter, they'd still give him the side-eye.

What the hell had happened to his life?

After disconnecting the call with Eleanora's mother, he called the head of security for Grand York.

"Do you have any way of finding out if someone is on a flight?"

His chief of security, Brandon Feathers, said, "What?"

"Eleanora is returning to Rome. She didn't take the company jet." He forced himself to sound professional and detached. "Meaning she's on a commercial flight. I want to know when she's arriving in Rome. So I—"

Damn it. He couldn't think of anything to say. He'd taken it one step too far. He should have stopped at wanting to know when she was arriving.

"So you can call her?"

"Yes. Sorry. It's so close to Christmas that my head's going in too many directions."

Brandon laughed. "Don't I know it. I still don't have a gift for my wife."

"You've got a couple of days."

Brandon's laugh got louder. "You're such a newbie. If you don't get a gift by like the twenty-third all the good stuff is picked over. You can't do things last minute."

For some reason or another that stuck Marco oddly. He didn't have a gift for his dad. He didn't have a Christmas gift for Eleanora either—

No. It wasn't the Christmas gifts bothering him. It was the words *last minute*. He'd waited until she was angry with him before he'd seen the light. It probably *did* look like he'd only asked her to marry him because he thought he had to.

"Give me a second and I'll get the manifest."

"You can do that?"

"Yeah. Just give me a couple of minutes."

He hung up the phone and waited. When Brandon called back, he gave Marco Eleanora's flight number and departure time.

He thanked him and hung up the phone. Sunrise looked up at him. Sunset sat up on the sofa.

"Yes. I'm going after her." He looked at the time. "But I'm not going to catch her at the airport." He dialed the number for his pilot. "I'm going to get to Rome first because my jet is faster."

Not sure how long he would be staying, Marco quickly packed a bag and was downstairs in fifteen minutes. Sam awaited him. He opened the door and Marco slid inside.

As Sam pulled out, Chiara texted him. Three days until Vermont.

He groaned. All this time he'd worried Chiara would be the one to disappoint their father but maybe it was going to be him.

He answered Chiara. She sent him a smiley face. And he squeezed his eyes shut. No one in his family had any idea the mess his life had become.

Sam got him to the private airstrip housing his jet and the pilots were already there, the jet on the tarmac ready to leave.

He really would get to Rome before Eleanora did.

He boarded the jet, suddenly tired, and glad

he could nap as the pilots flew him across the Atlantic. Forcing himself to remember he wanted to be rested when he got to Rome, he talked himself into letting his brain go blank and falling asleep.

His jet landed and within seconds his phone rang. Thinking it was Chiara, answering his text with a call, he glanced at caller ID, and groaned. Not only was his dad calling but he was video calling.

With a long drink of air, he clicked to answer. "Hey, Dad!"

"Hey, Marco. Just calling to see what time you're getting here on the twenty-third."

"I'm really not sure."

His dad's expression dissolved into confused unhappiness. "Not sure?"

"I mean I'll be there." He hoped. "I'm just not sure what time."

"Really, because I would think that would be something that would be easy to figure out."

"It's complicated." If he thought telling his dad he'd gotten Eleanora pregnant was going to be difficult, explaining that he convinced her they shouldn't get married, but now he wanted to marry her, and she didn't believe him would be doubly so.

Hell, sometimes he didn't understand it himself.

His dad continued talking. The whole time Marco could hear nervousness in his voice. He decided his dad was simply worried that his kids were going to bail on him for Christmas Eve *again*. But he couldn't say anything to assure him that wouldn't happen. After an awkward minute or two, they disconnected the call.

He got off the jet, shaking his head. His life was a mess, but his family was a bigger mess. They hadn't had a Christmas together in three years and when they finally decide to see each other it was as if they couldn't do it.

Because they hadn't dealt with his mother's death?

He almost stopped walking.

They *hadn't* dealt with his mother's death. None of them had.

Recognition fluttered through him. He could see that now. Not because time had passed but because falling in love with Eleanora for real gave him the strength to see the truth.

He'd talked about his mom with her the day they'd danced in the lobby of the Grand York, and she'd told him things that had given him peace.

After ten years, he finally had peace about his mother's death.

He would always miss her, but that conversation with Eleanora had changed him. In these past weeks, he wasn't trying to figure things out so he and Eleanora could co-parent, he'd been falling in love. Not in the paper-thin way he'd always believed love to be, but in a deep, abiding way.

This was serious. *This* was love.

He was ready for everything he and Eleanora could have together. The way his mom would have wanted him to be.

Except he'd blown the proposal.

He knew she loved him. He loved her—

He thought back to the words he said the night he'd asked her to marry him. Everything about him and Eleanora had always been easy and fun, and he'd made that proposal flat and inelegant.

He'd wanted to fix it. He'd tried to come up with a way to ask her to marry him again that would show her that he loved her, but he hadn't. He wasn't any good at real love. She'd be crazy to take him back, crazy to even listen to another proposal.

He stopped walking. If he kept pursuing a woman who was now hell-bent on getting away from him, he was the one who was going to end up hurt.

His limo driver opened the passenger door. Obviously having been apprised of why he was in Rome, he said, "I can drive you to the airport, sir."

"Do you know if her flight has landed?"

"Yes. But they haven't deplaned."

"They haven't?"

"Gates are crowded."

"Then let's get going!"

He waited for his brain to go nuts with warnings about being hurt but nothing came except a reminder that *she* was hurt. He'd hurt her. And he couldn't have that. It was his job to love her. She was his.

His brain stumbled. She *was* his. She had always been his. This was what she'd been waiting for, for him to have the overwhelming realization not just that they belonged together but that his life without her was intolerable. That she made him laugh and think and they were amazing together in bed.

As they drove to the airport, he realized he had always loved her. It had taken until now to recognize she was his. For real. Forever. No matter what. By God, that's what he intended to tell her.

The risk of it whispered through him. He'd always controlled the things in his life that he could control and handled the unexpected. But he suddenly saw that life was nothing without risk and even less than nothing without love. That was what his dad had been going through. That's what their family had been going through. Emptiness caused by fear or loss.

Well, he was done being afraid and living half a life.

CHAPTER SIXTEEN

ELEANORA SAT IN her coach seat, waiting to be allowed to deplane. Due to holiday travel, the tarmac was crowded. Gates were all full. They couldn't get out of the plane until the plane had been assigned a gate. Right now, there was no gate open to assign.

There was no point to being antsy.

She had a moment of sighing at her impatience and had to remind herself that she didn't belong with the crowd that had private jets.

Marco did though. Strong, handsome, always smart Marco fit that life. A wave of missing him overtook her but she told herself she was doing the right thing by setting him free.

She glanced out the window. It was cold but sunny. Still, it didn't have the feeling of New York. There was nowhere like New York around Christmas. She thought back to watching skaters with Marco, dancing romantically around the Christmas tree in the Grand York, even walking the cats in the flurries. Tears filled her eyes.

She told herself she wasn't crying because she would miss him or because they'd missed their chance at something wonderful, but because she was sentimental about Christmas and New York City.

When their plane finally got a gate, she rose to get her small suitcase and walked out of the plane and into the airport concourse. Rome was her home now. It wasn't New York, but that was for the best. She needed to be away from New York. She needed to be away from Marco.

She pressed her hand to her tummy. It was her and her baby against the world now.

Except when Marco had custody. She wouldn't deny him the chance to know and love his child.

Sadness rippled through her. She wanted him to love her too. But she was going to have to get beyond that. He loved her like a friend, even wanted to try to love her as more if his proposal was anything to go by, but he couldn't. If being with him had taught her nothing else, she'd realized she deserved for someone to love her madly. She might have thought for a fleeting second that she'd never find that love, but it didn't matter. If she had to spend the rest of her life searching for it, she would.

No more hopeless attitude about love. She swore to God she would find it.

Her heart stumbled when she thought about

giving up on Marco and she accepted it would take some time to get over him. But she'd also decided to give herself the entire holiday to wallow in the grief of losing him. Then she'd force herself to be strong and move on.

She retrieved her luggage in baggage claim and headed for the door. With her head down, looking at her phone so she could call for a ride, she saw a swatch of fabric almost on the floor—

Someone's trousers?

At ground level?

Kneeling?

She stopped before she ran into the guy. She lifted her head enough to see Marco kneeling in front of her, that damned ring box in his hands.

"I know I did this all wrong the first time."

Her heart wanted to squeeze at the sweetness of the gesture, but she also knew Marco was a planner and a hard worker. If he made a mistake, he studied what he'd done until he could fix it.

"Get up."

"No. I'm not letting you go! You are the woman I want in my life. It took you leaving before I realized that."

Her heart did squeeze. But she reminded herself that what he saw as love, what he wanted in his life as love, was a shallow version of what she wanted.

"I flew here, nearly was in an accident racing

to the airport to catch you, so I could tell you that I'm lost without you."

She swallowed hard. That one was hard to ignore.

"Not because we fit but because there are ways we don't fit. We always laughed about those things. Now I see they are what make us…well, us. These past few weeks have been too wonderful to put into words."

Her chest tightened with the need to believe that.

"We blended together so easily that I didn't realize how special it was—how wonderful it was—to fall in love with my best friend. My heart doesn't want to beat without you. My life is empty. The penthouse is cold and lifeless. What I thought was a life is only an existence. You bring the life into my world."

The tears she'd been holding back spilled over and he rose.

He shoved the ring box into his jacket pocket and took her hands. "I don't know why I couldn't see it. Maybe it was because we did click so easily. But I adore you. I want to marry you. Not because we're going to have our child. Because you fill my world with happiness." He took a breath. "I had to make a trip to Italy and walk through airports and endure a long limo ride before I saw how unhappy my world had been."

Ready to burst into ugly sobs, she said nothing. He reached into his jacket pocket and got the ring out again. He pulled it from the box and slipped it on her finger.

"I like to think I make you happy too."

With great effort, she whispered, "You do."

He squeezed his eyes shut with relief, leaned in and kissed her. For the first time, passion mixed and mingled with an emotion that went beyond anything she'd ever felt. As the warmth of love surged through her, her stomach fluttered.

At first, she thought it was happiness and hormones, but it fluttered again.

With a gasp, she pulled back. "The baby moved."

"What?"

"The baby moved!" She put his hand on her stomach as the little flutters she'd felt continued.

"Well, I'll be damned."

She laughed. "I think he or she approves."

"Either that or my timing is impeccable."

She laughed again and rose to brush a quick kiss across his lips. "Our timing sucks. Our timing has always sucked. But for the first time, I have the sense that we're getting it right."

"Does this mean you're not going to give back the ring? That we're engaged?"

She took a long breath, as her shock receded,

and her world righted. This man whom she loved, loved her too. "You bet your boots it does."

He took the handle of her suitcase from her hand and turned toward the exit. "That might go down as the world's silliest proposal acceptance."

She stopped, putting her hand on his forearm to stop him too. "All those things you said about how you feel about me? That's how I've felt about you for a couple of years. I adore you. I don't want another man. I want you. For you. Not for any reason other than I love you."

He smiled and kissed her again. "That's a lot better."

"Surely you didn't have doubts."

"You flat out refused my first proposal. And I was offering the best-looking ring in recorded history."

"But you didn't yet realize that you loved me, and I couldn't accept anything less."

He studied her for a second. "No. I don't suppose you could." People waiting for bags had gotten them and were headed to the same door that Marco and Eleanora stood in front of. The crowd ebbed and flowed around them.

"What do you say? Want to get back on the jet and go home?"

She winced. "I'd really like a shower first."

He laughed. "We could spend the night at the Grand York."

"And have our employees be the first to know we're engaged?" She motioned for him to walk through the door. "How about if we stay at the competitor, have breakfast in bed tomorrow morning and head straight to Vermont?"

"Sounds like a plan."

"That way your dad will be the first to know."

He smiled. "I think he'd approve."

"I think your mom would approve too."

And just like that Marco felt like himself, the man he was supposed to be, but couldn't be because his life had gotten confused. Grief had caused him to believe real love didn't exist and being so busy had kept him from having enough time to realize it wasn't true.

But in a way, he was glad things had worked out the way they had. He and Eleanora had always belonged together. They'd always loved each other, taken care of each other. The ring he'd given her only made official what she seemed to have always known.

They were meant to share their lives.

EPILOGUE

Six months later, on a blistering hot day in Manhattan, Eleanora gave birth to an eight-pound boy.

Marco laughed joyfully and kissed her forehead before walking to the end of the birthing table to see his son. "My mother always said big babies ran in our family."

"I wish you had told me that before we got involved."

The doctor laughed. "There is some genetics to this, but no one can really predict what combination of people will produce a big baby."

"And for all we know, big babies run in your family too."

"I'll ask my mom."

"Oh, did she and your dad get here?"

The nurse walked over with his son, cleaned up and wrapped in a blanket. He saw the scrunched-up face and tears filled his eyes. He walked back to Eleanora. "And here he is."

Her face filled with awe as she took their son. "Oh, my goodness. Robert?"

Marco winced. "Too formal."

"Oh, my goodness, Toby?"

"Too much like a kid's toy."

"Oh, my goodness, Antonio…" Her voice trailed off hopefully.

"You'd think in nine months we'd have decided on a name."

Having removed his gloves and washed his hands, the doctor walked to the top of the bed. He shook Marco's hand. "Congratulations." He caught Eleanora's gaze. "And to you. We'll see you next baby."

Eleanora said, "Yes. Thank you for everything, you've been wonderful, Gabe."

Marco blinked. He glanced at the doctor's name tag, Gabriel Montgomery. They'd talked about Gabriella as a name if the baby was a girl. But they'd never thought of Gabriel for a boy.

He rolled it around in his head. He could see little Gabe Pearson at six catching a baseball, at eight learning to skateboard, at sixteen taking shifts as a waiter in the Grand York's restaurant to learn the family business from the ground up.

The doctor slapped Marco on the shoulder before he walked out of the room.

Marco leaned down to touch his son's soft cheek. "What do you think of Gabriel?"

"Our doctor?"

"No. Other version of Gabriella."

She inhaled a small gasp. "Your mom's name but for a boy?"

"Gabriel when he takes the reins of the company and Gabe when he's a kid and with family."

She laughed. "I think it's perfect."

He kissed her forehead. "So do I." He leaned back enough that he could take the baby from her arms. "Welcome to the world, Gabriel Pearson."

* * * * *

Look out for the next story in the
A Five-Star Family Reunion trilogy
Christmas with His Ballerina
by Jessica Gilmore.

Coming soon!

And if you enjoyed this story,
check out these other great reads
from Susan Meier

His Majesty's Forbidden Fling
The Single Dad's Italian Invitation
Reunited Under the Mistletoe

All available now!